Bec

(Circa 1985)

W. Eggleston

Paper back ISBN: 979-8-9996190-0-6

Ebook ISBN: 979-8-9996190-1-3

Library of Congress Control Number: 2025921597

Literary Fiction: A novel about obsession

A faded, decades-old photograph and the fleur-de-lis tattoo. Not much to go on. Can this really be the man Clay was paid to find by the woman with the hyacinth scent? How long can he keep up the charade, and what happens if he's discovered? Clay Trinian finds himself skating on very thin ice as dark obsessions swirl around a South Jersey shore town of the mid-1980s. Clay wants Sylvie; Sylvie wants Bec. But then everyone wants Bec.

Contents

*For Steve, who has always believed in me.
And for Anechy without whom this book might have
never seen the light.*

CHAPTER I

The walls were an indefinite pastel, blue perhaps, dulled by years of Uncle Bert's thick cigar smoke. The whole room reflected Uncle Bert's person. Everything tidy, nothing really out of place, and yet a sense of dinginess. Neat, but not clean. Only the very barest essentials here in the office: desk and chair, chair for clients, beat-up file cabinets, old school-room clock, and a calendar that had obviously been given away free as an advertising gimmick. No pictures, no mirrors, no couch, no carpet, not even a coat tree, only a bare wire coat hanger hooked over one of the file cabinet drawer handles. Just like Uncle Bert. Always a plain brown suit and shoes, white shirt and dark, nondescript tie. No tie clasp, no belt, nothing unnecessary, except those god-awful, omnipresent cigars. Clay could remember his father, Bert's brother, kidding about their being "El Ropo" brand. The smell hung in every corner of the tiny office. Not even a lousy book or magazine to look at. Clay turned the old swivel desk chair toward the window. It creaked and screamed as if it didn't know it could turn in that direction. Mid-afternoon, mid-week, not much happening out on the street. Clay was wondering what his uncle would do if he had more than one client visit at a time as there was only one available chair when the office door opened. At first he thought it must be Uncle Bert back from his one o'clock appointment. When he realized it wasn't, he nearly knocked over the old swivel chair jumping up to speak to the woman who had just entered the room.

She came in timidly as if not sure she had the right office, but she had to have seen the dark, spare lettering on the door: 'Berton G. Trinian—Confidential Investigations'.

"Mr. Trinian?" she asked, a half-surprised, half-embarrassed look on her face.

"Yes—that is, I'm Clay Trinian—I'm not Bert Trinian—he's my uncle." Why was he stammering like an idiot? She had just caught him so off-guard.

"I know I should have called for an appointment, but I—well, I was hoping you might have time to see me this afternoon," she apologized moving closer to the desk.

'My God, she thinks I work here,' the thought flashed through Clay's mind. But it did sound better than the truth that he was just waiting for his uncle because he didn't have anything better to do with this afternoon. Maybe he could just get the information from her and relay it to his uncle.

"Do you have time?" she asked.

"Ah...yes, as a matter of fact I do have a little time before the next appointment," he smiled and showed her to the client chair in front of the desk. What a liar. Thank God she was alone, at least he wouldn't have to worry about the seating question.

"How long have you been working with your uncle?" she asked softly, nervously.

"Oh, several years," he answered. Why was he doing this? Sinking deeper.

"Actually I'm glad that you're here," she said in the same small voice. "I mean I'm sure your uncle is very competent—it's just that—I know this sounds silly, but I was afraid I might have to talk to some cigar-chomping, old man in a rumpled suit. I guess I've been watching too many movies."

They both laughed. If only she knew she had just described Uncle Bert perfectly.

"Anyway," she continued, "I think it will be easier for me to explain to someone younger—like you."

"I see," he tried his best to sound professional while retaining this young quality that seemed to please her. "Now, how can I help you?"

She looked down at her hands. He could see her eyes moving beneath the dark lashes. 'She's beautiful,' he thought to himself suddenly. 'No, not beautiful exactly—she's...captivating. Yes, that's it—captivating, in its true sense.'

She looked up at him, suddenly remembering, "I'm sorry, I forgot to introduce myself didn't I? My name is Sylvie Daros."

He nodded for her to continue.

"I'm sure this is very routine for you—it's just a little difficult—I've never done anything like this before."

'If only she knew,' Clay thought, but tried to put her at ease and asked her to go on.

"I want you to find someone for me."

Clay felt as if he, too, had been watching too many movies. A wandering husband? A boyfriend who had disappeared under suspicious circumstances?

"Have you tried the police? I mean if this is a missing persons case," he tried to think of what Uncle Bert might ask her.

"No, it's not that, he's not missing—I mean I don't know where he is, but it's not that he's a missing person. This is somewhat difficult to explain."

"Please, take your time," he said although he was afraid his uncle might appear at any moment and put an end to this charade. 'Why am I doing this?' he asked himself, but he seemed unable to stop.

"I want you to find a man named Billy—William—Becton," she paused and drew in a deep breath. It was as though speaking this man's name aloud had broken some sort of spell. She spoke more quickly now, still guarded, but more easily than before. "I want you to find him—but he mustn't know anything about this."

"You mean I find him and let you know, then you can run into him like a chance meeting?"

"Oh, no—no!" A look of genuine horror crossed her face at this suggestion. "I don't want to see him—I mean I don't want him to know that I'm looking for him. I just want to know where he is, that he's all right, that he's happy. Is he happy? I must know. That's the important thing—that he's happy. Do you understand?" She glanced away quickly, trying to control her growing agitation.

He nodded and smiled faintly, but he wasn't sure that he did understand, not really. He asked her to continue anyway. As she spoke he studied her from across the desk, trying to remember the things Uncle Bert was always telling him about people and their motives. Sylvie—the name seemed to fit her. Small, vulnerable, yet something slightly threatening about the eyes. The dark lashes—little flashes every now and then—like some small, cornered animal looking for a way out.

Clay listened as she went on with her story—a brief teenage romance with this Becton that had left an inexplicably deep mark. Her soft voice changed when she spoke of him—controlled— deliberately controlled as if trying to hide some private desperation.

"I know it must sound silly to you, my wanting to find him after all this time, but I really have to know and I couldn't hire anyone before this."

She was so obviously nervous about being here in this office, about having put herself in this situation, opening up such a secret to a total stranger. Her need to know about the condition of this Becton must have been tremendous to overcome her apparently innate reserve.

"I'm afraid there's really not very much I can tell you that will help in finding him. I do have this picture, but it's very old. He may not look anything like that now. I would like to have the picture back when you're done?" "She handed the small photograph carefully across the desk. "There's a sample of his handwriting on the back, if that will help."

A light floral scent breached the oppressive cigar smell as she reached across the desk to indicate the scribbling on the back of the picture. Hyacinths?

Turning his attention to the photograph, Clay found it to be an unremarkable picture of a young man in his late teens—tall, thin, dark. Judging from his clothing and the length of his hair the photo had probably been taken during the late sixties. The message on the back seemed equally as mundane except for a small design which appeared directly beneath the signature. Clay recognized it as a somewhat stylized fleur-de-lis. He asked Sylvie about it.

"Oh, yes," she laughed softly. "Billy had this thing about ancestry, family trees. He found out that his ancestors on his mother's side were French—generations ago. Anyway, it seemed to mean a lot to him. He started signing his letters with a fleur-de-lis like that."

"Ah, I see," Clay said, trying to remember that Becton had been a teenager at the time.

"The only other thing I can tell you is that Billy was going to Morgan College here in Pennsylvania—a sophomore—the last time I heard from him. That was October, 1969."

Clay wasn't sure which intrigued him more, Sylvie or her story about Billy Becton. Hyacinths. He knew he wanted to see her again.

"Can you help me? Can you find him for me?" she asked.

He would of course never be able to find this guy, but he could make a show of trying—just to be able to see her again. Taking her money under false pretenses? Hell, he'd give her back the money, say he'd done the best he could, and well, they could take it from there.

"Yes, I'm sure we can help you," he said. It was too late to turn back now. "Is there a number where I can reach you?"

"No," she said quickly, "I mean I'd rather see you in person. Shall I come back here?"

"No," Clay had to think fast, "no, let's meet for lunch. I'll let you know what I've found out. A week from today, 2:00 at Mallary's—do you know where that is?"

"Yes, I think so—I'll find it anyway. A week from today. Thank you so much. You really think you'll be able to find him?"

"We'll do our best," he assured her as he followed her to the door, "I'm sure I'll have some news for you by next week," he added as the door closed.

It all seemed so possible, so necessary—this colossal lie—while she was there—but now that he was alone in the office again...'My God,' he thought, 'what have I done? Better yet, what am I going to do next?'

Before he could get his bearings, the door opened again. A large cloud of gray smoke announced his uncle's return.

"So, who was the lady with the dark hair I just saw leaving here?" he asked Clay.

"So, who was she?" Uncle Bert repeated when Clay returned only a blank stare to his first question.

"Ah, uh—a client," Clay finally managed.

"So how come she didn't stick around 'til I got back? Was she in that big a hurry?"

"Well, sort of."

"What's all this about anyway?" Uncle Bert asked, working the fat cigar between his teeth. "You finally decided you want to work with me?"

His uncle had suggested this many times, but Clay had never really taken him seriously. Now, it seemed like a perfect way out.

"As a matter of fact, I might like to work with you—on this case anyway."

"Yeah, what's so special about this case?"

"I don't know—it just seems like it might be interesting."

"Uh-huh. Remember Rule No.1: Don't get personally involved with the clients. She seems a little old for you anyway, you know?"

"Right—I just thought it might be interesting. Besides, I haven't got anything better to do with my time right now." Clay knew this last statement was all too true.

"Your mother been after you again about finding a steady job?"

"Some things never change." Clay knew his mother had never been thrilled about having a private detective in the family even if only by marriage. As if to deliberately irritate her, Bert had always fostered his youngest nephew's interest in the business. Clay's visits over the years to his uncle's office in Philadelphia had been prompted as much by a need to escape from his parents and older brothers as by an interest in the P.I. trade.

"Okay. Fine. So what's her problem?"

"She wants us to find this guy," Clay handed him the old photograph. "That picture was taken over fifteen years ago."

"What's she want him for—alimony, child support?"

"No, at least I don't think so..."

"You mean you didn't ask her."

"No, but I really don't think that's it. Anyway, she doesn't want us to let him know that she's looking for him."

"Child support. Mark my words. Child support."

"Well, anyway, what do we do first?"

"You mean, what do you do first. If this case interests you so much, you can do the work on it. Did you take any notes while you were talking to her?"

Clay shook his head.

"First, you have to get organized. Now write down everything she told you about this guy," Uncle Bert pushed a yellow pad and pencil across the desk toward Clay.

Clay listed: William (Billy) Becton

Present age approx. 35

Last known address: Morgan College

"That's it?" his uncle frowned.

"'Fraid so," Clay didn't think that Becton's being a Francophile would be of any help.

"That's not much to go on, but there's nothing like a challenge."

"You mean you think you might actually be able to find this guy?"

"No, I mean you might be able to find him. Did she give you her phone number?"

"No, just her name."

"So she's going to come back here?"

"Uh, no—I'm meeting her for lunch next week."

His uncle studied him for a moment between puffs on the stubby cigar. "Be careful kid, don't get in over your head."

Clay guessed his uncle's years in the business had indeed taught him something of people and their motives.

CHAPTER II

Clay sat on the edge of the narrow bed, his elbows on his knees, his head supported by his hands blocking out the glare from the bare overhead bulb. His shoulders ached and the inside of his head felt raw. Sleep. He had to sleep.

'Maybe if I just lie down for a few minutes—then I'll get up, get undressed, brush my teeth, then go back to bed properly...' he thought as he swung his legs onto the thin mattress. Why? How had he ever gotten involved in this?

The clattering of dishes in Uncle Bert's kitchenette awakened Clay. What time was it? It couldn't be too late if his uncle were still here fixing breakfast. Clay glanced at his watch. It had stopped at 3:00. He guessed from the light filtering through the old venetian blinds that it must be about 8:00. Surprisingly, his clothes did not appear that rumpled for having been slept in. He had been so dead-tired he figured he must not have moved much during the night.

The raw feeling in his head had diminished somewhat, but Clay could sense a dull throb working at the back of his neck. He shuffled toward the bathroom. Aspirin and a shower. He couldn't force himself to think beyond that. His mind began to work as he leaned against the wall of the narrow shower stall. The hot water beat at his shoulders making tiny rivulets through the auburn hair as it rolled down his chest. He lingered under the hot water, mostly because it felt so good, but also because he was hoping to avoid his uncle. Clay knew that if he waited until after 8:30 to emerge from the bathroom he could count on having the little apartment to himself. It wasn't that he didn't really want to talk to his uncle. He didn't really want to talk to anyone this morning—and the hot water felt so good. Clay thought back over the past week.

Thursday—the day after his meeting with Sylvie—he had driven west from the city to Tilton where Morgan College was located. Clay had taken his uncle's advice and waited until lunchtime to stage his assault on the alumni office. After asking half-a -dozen people, students mostly, he finally managed to find the small office. In a corner on the top floor of the administration building, it wasn't a place that most of the current campus residents had much to do with. Uncle Bert knew what he was talking about. At noon the regular secretary left for lunch and a student took over at the reception desk of the little office. Luckily the student was young, inexperienced, and female, probably a freshman or sophomore. She became very flustered when Clay approached the desk and inquired about William Becton. He took advantage of the young girl's nervousness. Pouring on the southern charm and posing as the younger brother of one of Becton's old school friends, Clay persuaded her that he was in a hurry and really couldn't wait for the regular secretary's return. After some cajoling and flattery and assurance that this would be their little secret, she handed over the home address they had on file for Becton. Driving away from the campus, Clay felt more than a little ashamed of the way he had manipulated the young girl. But at the same time there was a certain feeling of power at having been able to get what he wanted with relative ease. But that was just the beginning.

The address Clay had gotten from Morgan College was in northeastern Maryland and was that of Becton's parents or rather had been. Posing this time as a long-lost cousin, Clay learned from neighbors that Mrs. Becton had moved to Wilmington, Delaware. They weren't sure what had happened to Mr. Becton after the divorce. And Billy—one said he'd gone out West, another thought maybe he'd gone to Canada. Wonderful! At this point Clay had returned to his uncle's office.

Uncle Bert pulled open the deep right-hand bottom drawer of his desk. It contained telephone directories for many of the major cities and key suburban areas within a wide radius of Philadelphia. After shuffling through them for a few seconds he pulled one out for Wilmington, Delaware.

"Okay," he said between puffs on his cigar, "the best lead you've got at this point is the mother. At least you have something to go on." He handed the phone book to Clay.

Clay thumbed through the B's as his uncle rummaged through the map drawer in one of the old file cabinets. Clay didn't know the woman's first name but it turned out there was only one Becton listed—H. Becton. He prayed she didn't have an unlisted number.

"What's the address?" Uncle Bert asked unfolding a map of Wilmington. Without waiting for an answer, he looked over Clay's shoulder, found the address and began tracing on the map with his stubby index finger. "Well, what're you waiting for? Aren't you going to call her?"

Clay was eager to find out if this H. Becton was indeed Billy's mother, but he was somewhat hesitant to display his investigative technique in front of his uncle. Not having had any formal training, Clay had so far been going on instinct and hazy memories of old movies and TV P.I.'s. He wasn't sure what his uncle's reaction would be—but he dialed anyway.

"Hello, Mrs. Becton?...My name is Al Johnson. I'm trying to get in touch with your son, Billy. We were friends back at Morgan College. He told me if I was ever in the area to give him a call." Clay waited, trying to catch his breath.

"I'm sorry, Mrs. Becton isn't here. You say you're a friend of Billy's?" It sounded like an older woman on the other end of the line.

"Yes, we knew each other at school. Do you know where I can reach him?"

"Well, let me see, Harriet told me he was living somewhere at the shore."

"The shore?" Clay was growing somewhat desperate.

"Yes, the Jersey Shore—I think it was somewhere near Atlantic City."

"But you don't know the name of the town?"

"No, I'm afraid not."

"Is there any way I can talk to Mrs. Becton? I'd really like to get in touch with Billy and I won't be in this area for very long."

"No, Harriet won't be back for another month. Listen, I've got to go now. Somewhere near Atlantic City—I'm sure that's what she said."

The line went dead. Clay stared at the pad he'd been scribbling on during the call. The only words he had written were shore and Atlantic City. He had gotten so involved in the conversation that he had forgotten about his uncle. Now, a low chuckle brought him back.

"Al Johnson?" his uncle laughed. "I don't know about you, kid. So, what'd you find out?"

Clay held the scratch pad up for his uncle to read.

"So he's in Atlantic City?"

"No, he might be somewhere near Atlantic City. Mrs. Becton wasn't there. I talked to some friend of hers. That was the best she could do."

"When is Mrs. Becton going to be home?"

"Not for a month. Got any suggestions?"

"Hmm...I'd say go to Wilmington. See if any of the neighbors can give you something more definite," Uncle Bert handed Clay the map, pointing to the Bectons' neighborhood.

Following his uncle's advice, the next morning Clay set out for Wilmington. He spent the better part of the day trudging from door to door, but the neighbors who would talk to him seemed to know even less than the woman he had spoken to on the phone.

"Well, looks like you're going to the shore," Uncle Bert smiled when Clay told of his disappointing day.

Monday and Tuesday were a blur of highway, beachfront, and phone booths. For some reason Uncle Bert had insisted that Clay check out the shore lead in person. Probably to get him out from under foot in the office. Clay had started with Atlantic City itself, just in case. There were two Bectons listed in the Atlantic City phone book, but neither of them knew anything about Billy. On the flip of a coin, Clay started working his way south along the coast. In each of the small towns marked on the map, Clay stopped at a phone booth and checked the local directory. He found a Becton listed in two of the towns but they both proved to be dead ends.

***

Clay turned off the shower. His uncle must have left for the office by now. He opened the bathroom door slowly. The little apartment was quiet and more to the point—smokeless. His uncle was gone. Clay sat at the small, round table positioned strategically between the living room and kitchenette. He tried to read the morning paper his uncle had left behind as he lingered over his coffee and toast. But now that he was fully awake, Clay could think of nothing but Sylvie.

During the week since his first meeting with Sylvie, Clay had tried to focus on finding Billy Becton. The search and ensuing fatigue had been the predominant features of the last few days. But always in the back of his mind he held the thought that on Wednesday he would see her again. Now, sitting in his uncle's apartment with only a few hours until that meeting, Clay allowed himself the indulgence of letting her flood into his thoughts.

The sound of a siren on the street below brought him out of his reverie. It was already almost ten o'clock. For the next couple of hours Clay busied himself with laundry and vacuuming the apartment as he had promised his uncle he would. The memory of the vulnerability in Sylvie's voice and the scent of hyacinths stayed with him as he went about his chores. Throughout the morning Clay had experienced a growing sense of excitement—anticipation. It wasn't the thought of making a report on his first case or even the fact that he didn't have anything definite to report. It was Sylvie. His mind played over her name. 'My God,' he thought, 'I'm acting like a teenager.' He tried to calculate the difference between their ages. Sylvie couldn't be more than a couple years younger than Becton—say thirty-three. So maybe about seven years between them. That wasn't really so much, was it?

CHAPTER III

Clay had dressed slowly, carefully for the meeting but still arrived at Mallary's too early. He walked around the block twice trying to kill time. Finally he entered the restaurant, still five minutes early. The hostess seated him right away. As he had hoped, most of the lunch crowd had already cleared out. So far, so good. He had been shown to a table at the far side of the main room, against the wall. Clay was grateful. He hated being out in the middle of the room. Today it seemed especially important that he be in a comfortable position—perhaps to try to retain some sort of control over what might transpire—better yet, control over himself. He fidgeted with the silverware and glanced incessantly at his watch. 'Oh my God,' he was struck suddenly, 'what if she doesn't show up?' The thought had never entered his mind until that instant. He felt as if he had stopped just short of a deep chasm—staring down into the darkness when he was rescued by a small lavender form moving toward him. He managed to compose himself just in time to jump up and seat Sylvie across the table.

She seemed even slighter, more delicate than at their first meeting. She apologized for being late but offered no excuses nor explanations. Clay made a pretense of studying his menu while Sylvie looked at hers. In reality he had already decided on his order and he used this time to take in Sylvie. He could manage only short, furtive glances when he was sure she wasn't looking. Short glances, like brief photographic frames that he quickly assembled in his mind. Lavender. A pale lavender suit. Linen suit. White, silky blouse. Soft bow at the neck. On anyone else the pale lavender might have seemed slightly out of season now in mid-September, but it suited her perfectly—her pale skin, her dark hair.

Although she seemed somewhat more at ease than at their first meeting, Sylvie ate very little of her lunch. She cut small segments from the garden omelet with the side of her fork and picked at them absently as they talked. She tried to initiate polite conversation—remarks about the weather and the traffic—but Clay knew she was eager for news of Becton. He reviewed the past week's search, trying to emphasize its disappointments and drudgery. Clay ended his report stressing that he would be back on the job again tomorrow combing the phone directories of seaside towns. He had hoped that Sylvie would not be too upset at his not having found Becton in a week. On the contrary, she seemed positively hopeful.

"The shore," she whispered almost to herself, then in a normal tone of voice, "I had forgotten how much Billy loved the shore."

Clay wished she had remembered this at their first meeting, but he couldn't be angry with her.

"Do you know if there was any place in particular—any towns he especially liked?"

"Yes, there was Avalon and Sea Isle City and sometimes Trident Beach," Sylvie replied eagerly, "and you did check Atlantic City?"

Clay assured her that he had as he quickly wrote down the names of the other three towns in a pocket notebook.

As the waitress brought more coffee, Sylvie checked her wristwatch. She seemed suddenly alarmed, asking Clay if it were really three-thirty. She quickly took a long, white envelope from her purse and handed it across the table.

"That's for the first week and next week. Thank you for all you've done," she said hurriedly. "Please keep looking. I'm sorry I really have to go. Can we meet here again next week for lunch—same time?"

"Yes, that will be fine." This sudden haste had caught him off-balance. Before he had a chance to think if there were anything else he wanted to ask, she was gone. He fought an impulse to run after her and sat down instead to finish his coffee. Now, alone at the table, the image that lingered in Clay's mind was the ornate ring he had noticed when Sylvie handed him the envelope. Lacy, silver filigree with a dark, opaque stone in the middle. In the glance he had gotten it appeared to be very old and perhaps of Spanish design. He hadn't noticed the ring at their first meeting but then he hadn't been looking. Somehow it had not occurred to him that she might be married. But was she? It really had not looked like a wedding ring and yet it was on the correct finger. Still puzzling over it, Clay opened the envelope she had given him. Expecting to find a check, he was surprised to see the full amount in cash—new bills, large denominations. Why hadn't she just written a check?

CHAPTER IV

Clay got an early start the next morning, trying to avoid his uncle's questions as he hurried out of the apartment. He decided it would be less hassle to get breakfast somewhere along the way. He had given Uncle Bert the business's percentage of Sylvie's payment and still had a tidy sum left to himself. It felt good to have a little extra cash and to be able to fill up his car for a change instead of just buying a couple dollars worth of gas at a time. At least Clay didn't have to feel guilty about taking Sylvie's money under false pretenses. He felt that he'd really earned it with all his running around looking for Billy Becton. He still felt strange about taking the money from her, not guilty exactly, but something else.

The first town Sylvie had suggested turned out to be a dead end as far as Becton was concerned, but it had a great place for a late breakfast. The second town also proved to be Bectonless. Only Trident Beach remained of the names Sylvie had given him. Clay checked his map. He hesitated before pulling back onto the highway. In a way he hoped that Trident Beach would be the place because the alternative was more uncertain trudging from town to town. At the same time he realized that the search for Billy Becton was his link to Sylvie. Once he found Becton, then what?

It was a beautiful day—sunny and warm. Even the slight breeze seemed unseasonably mild. Clay tried to focus on this as he started on the short drive to Trident Beach. It was after noon when he reached the center of town. This one, like all the other shore towns he had seen in the past week had a semi-deserted, post-Labor Day look to it. The warm weather, however, had brought a few more people out and Clay had to wait to get at a public phone. Holding his breath, he thumbed to the B's. He let it out in a low whistle. There it was—Becton, H.. Billy's mother again? Some instinct told him not to call this time and he quickly copied down the address. He thought about having lunch first—prolonging the agony—but he wasn't really hungry and he knew he wouldn't be able to eat until he found out. Clay walked to a nearby gas station for directions, then returned to his car. There was that feeling—somewhere deep between his stomach and intestines—that feeling that accompanied such events as his first airplane flight alone, his first real date, and every exam he'd ever taken in school. The feeling grew as he drove toward the south end of town. But why should he feel so nervous now? For all he knew it might be just another dead end.

The house was located two blocks back from the beach in the 2700 block of Meridian Avenue, facing East and the ocean. Clay parked at the curb and walked slowly toward the house. It was a large two-story, white frame. In most respects it looked like a typical older shore house except that for some reason the builder had fancied large, round windows instead of the usual shape. They made the place look like a giant purple martin house.

Clay knocked on the front door. There was no response. Reluctant, he knew he had to try again. He was caught in mid-knock this time as the door flew open.

"Hi, sorry to keep you waiting—I was just making some lunch. You're here about the ad? Come on back to the kitchen, we can talk in there."

Clay, unable to get a word in, followed the tall figure down a dark, narrow corridor to the back of the house. He felt as if he had fallen down the rabbit hole. Ad? What ad? Could he bluff his way through this one?

Now in the sunny kitchen Clay got his first good look at the man who had answered the door. Becton? Clay tried to visualize the young man in Sylvie's old photograph. There were similarities, but after fifteen years Clay couldn't be sure. If it was Becton, he had filled out quite a bit from the slim youth in the photo, but mostly into muscle. The same dark, wavy hair—much shorter than in the picture, but still a little longer than was currently fashionable. His face was just a little too broad to be truly handsome, but if this were Becton, Clay could understand why Sylvie had been attracted to him. There was something in his bearing that demanded attention, but not in an arrogant or intimidating way—a natural charisma.

"You want some lemonade?" without waiting for an answer, the man poured some into a thick, faceted glass and handed it to Clay. Searching the cupboard for another drinking glass, all he was able to come up with was one of those oddly-shaped glasses used for sprouting flower bulbs.

"This will do," he said pouring lemonade into it, "beats having to wash one."

Clay noticed the fountain of dirty dishes cascading from one of the double sinks onto the counter top.

"So, you've come about the ad? I'll have to tell you I'm a little surprised."

"Ah, well..." Jesus—what ad? Clay hoped if he stalled, the talkative stranger would fill in some of the blanks.

"I mean, not that there's anything wrong with a guy having this kind of a job. It's just that I've always had women before."

Clay nodded hoping for more of a lead, wondering what he'd gotten himself into.

"Actually a guy just might work out better though," the man continued as if reasoning with himself. He smiled at Clay, "usually the ladies either think the stuff is disgusting and get offended or they get all heated up and want to get personally involved. You might be just what I need."

Clay was growing more apprehensive by the moment.

"So, how's your typing?" the man asked him.

"My typing?" Stunned, Clay burst into a short, nervous laugh. The stranger didn't seem to notice his discomfort and continued on.

"Yeah, speed's not too important. Accuracy is what I need and the main thing is that you can read my handwriting," he handed Clay a notebook page with some scribbling on it. "If you can believe it, my typing is even worse than that. That's why I have to hire someone."

Luckily for Clay, the cramped writing style closely resembled that of a college roommate and he was able to decipher the page without much difficulty. It looked similar to the handwriting on the back of Sylvie's photo, but he couldn't be sure. It was the content rather than the handwriting that captured Clay's attention. His eyebrows rose higher as he worked his way through it.

"So, you have any trouble reading it?" the man asked eagerly.

"Ah, no..." Clay answered still lingering over the page.

"Great! You don't find it offensive do you?"

"No, not offensive—titillating maybe."

"That's the idea," the man laughed. "I like to think of it as genteel pornography. It's really pretty trashy but my publisher tells me people are eating it up at the bookstands. And who am I to argue with public opinion or an advance check?" he laughed again and handed Clay a paperback from a stack of books on a shelf above the kitchen table.

The lurid title and cover illustration told of the book's contents. Clay thumbed through it as the man continued talking.

"It's racy enough to be commercial, but restrained enough to keep me out of jail—a fine line sometimes."

Clay looked again at the cover of the paperback and noticed the author's name—Becton Delacroix. "That's you?" Clay asked.

"Yeah—actually that's my 'nom de plume'," he answered, pronouncing the French words in an exaggerated manner. "Just call me Bec."

Becton! Clay's mind raced. But how could he be sure this was Billy and not a brother nor cousin. Sylvie hadn't mentioned anything about siblings.

"That's pretty much what the job entails—transcribing my handwriting into a legible form and some editing. How about some lunch? I can throw an extra hamburger on," Bec asked, changing subjects without changing gears. He opened a drawer in the refrigerator and took out the ground beef. He paused for a second and eyed Clay a bit suspiciously.

'The game is up,' thought Clay, but Bec spoke again before he could say anything.

"You're not a vegetarian or anything like that are you?" Bec asked.

"No, not a chance," Clay laughed with relief.

"Great! You've got the job!" Bec laughed, too, as he slapped the burgers into a large frying pan.

"Is that the only other job qualification?—Carnivore?"

"Yeah, maybe I should have included that in the ad. So—seriously—do you want the job? Two-hundred a week plus you can have a room upstairs if you need some place to stay."

"Sure, why not—sounds interesting," Clay answered handing the paperback to Bec. There was no time to think this through, but what better way to find out if this was really Billy Becton.

"Terrific! By the way, what's your name?"

"Clay Trinian."

"Clayton?"

"No, Barclay. Actually it's G. Barclay Trinian." What instinct made Clay give his real name?

Bec gave him a sidelong glance. "Were your parents expecting a banker?" he smiled.

"Yeah, I think that's what they were hoping for."

"What does the G. stand for?"

"Don't ask, please. Just call me Clay."

"Good enough. So, when can you get started, Clay?"

"How about tomorrow?"

"Perfect!"

"You say I can get a room upstairs?"

"Yeah, my mother runs this place as a rooming house during the summer but off-season like this you can have your choice of any room on the second floor except for No. 6—that's Mr. Suey's—he came with the place."

"That sounds great. I've been staying with a friend in Philly but it's getting a little crowded. I'll get packed up and be here tomorrow morning," Clay said as he bit into the hamburger Bec had placed before him on the table.

As he drove back to Uncle Bert's Clay tried to sort out his impressions of this 'Bec'. And the main question—was he Billy? He wished he could talk to Sylvie before he had to see Bec again but he knew that wasn't possible. There was no way of getting in touch with her until their lunch date next week.

Sylvie...Clay tried to put her out of his mind but she kept streaming back in during the drive to the city.

CHAPTER V

Clay wasn't sure how he was going to tell Uncle Bert about moving out but he knew there was no way of avoiding it. He was in the tiny spare bedroom packing when his uncle came home. Surprisingly, Bert asked few questions and offered no objections to the move. Maybe it wasn't such a surprise after all. The tiny apartment really wasn't big enough for the two men and although Bert hadn't said anything, Clay had a growing sense that he might be cramping his uncle's style. And, too, Uncle Bert was at the moment preoccupied with a juicy new case. At any rate, Clay was grateful for the hassle-free exit.

Early the next morning he loaded his car and started off for the shore. A light fog dusted the city but he guessed it might burn off by mid-morning. His first stop was Atlantic City to deliver some documents for his uncle, then he headed south toward Trident Beach. It was hard to believe that this was the same road he had travelled just a few days earlier in his search for Billy Becton. The desperate sprints from phone booth to phone booth had dulled his senses to the beauty of this drive south from Atlantic City. He drove slowly now, even below the speed limit at times, taking it all in. It wasn't the striking beauty of some vistas—not the stuff that post cards were made of. It was more a feeling. It had turned out to be a perfect September day—not too hot, but warm enough for shirtsleeves. The sun was out at full force now warming the light breeze coming off the ocean. It reflected off a dark-blue sky, white beach houses, and the greenish water he saw in flashes as he drove.

'God, it's good to be out of the city!' The thought struck Clay suddenly. The wide expanses—ocean, sand, long stretches of treeless, flat neighborhoods—got inside him. He felt new. The breeze from the open car window played on his neck. There was a sense of excitement that grew as he drove southward peaking as he reached Trident Beach. It was like the first day at a new school. Clay felt like laughing out loud and throwing up all at the same time. He knew he had to get a hold of himself before he saw Becton but he couldn't help it. This was the most alive he'd felt in...days? weeks? He pulled up to the curb in front of Becton's house parking behind a beat-up, dark-green Fiat. Clay wondered if the car belonged to Becton or if he had company. He glanced at the Fiat as he started up the walk. It wasn't as old as his own car, but was in much worse shape. Clay hoped it was Becton's; he wasn't really up for dealing with anyone else yet.

Clay knocked several times before the large front door swung open.

"Clay! Sorry, I was on the phone," Becton beamed as he reached for one of Clay's suitcases. "Hey, if you're going to be living here you don't need to knock anyway. I'll give you a key to the front door but it's usually unlocked," he called back over his shoulder as he led Clay up the stairs to the second floor. "The rooms up here are pretty good-sized. Take your pick—any one but No. 6—that's Mr. Suey's," he said pointing to a door at the far end of the corridor.

"Any suggestions?" Clay asked.

"How about No. 1? Lots of windows—corner room." Becton pointed to a room at the front of the house. "Closest thing we have to an ocean view," he added laughing.

"Sounds great."

Just as Becton got the door unlocked, they heard the muffled sound of a telephone ringing somewhere downstairs.

"Damn phone again! Go ahead and get settled in and then come on downstairs and we can get to work," Becton trailed off as he raced down the stairs toward the ringing.

Clay pushed the door open and entered slowly, letting his eyes adjust to the darkened room. Bed, dresser, small table and chair. 'My God!' Clay thought. 'If Uncle Bert and Becton's mother ever got together they could stage a minimalist coup.' Moving to the east wall he let the shades up on the two large, round windows. There was a swift transformation as the brilliant sunlight shot into the room. Clay hurried to roll up the shades on the south side. The house next door was a newer ranch style—only one story—leaving him an unimpeded view of deep-blue sky. Standing in the southeast corner, Clay surveyed the room, now filled with bright, yellow light.

It was hard to imagine the dark room he had entered just a few moments before and he vowed never to close the shades.

After unpacking a few things and walking around the room again he decided he'd stalled long enough and headed for the hallway. At the top of the stairs Clay drew in a deep breath. He guessed he was ready for the next encounter with Becton and he started down slowly.

Clay knocked lightly on the open living room door. From the other side of the room, Becton, still on the phone, motioned him through the doorway and into an old wing chair. Becton seemed to be doing more listening than talking, murmuring an "uh-huh" every now then. Clay took the opportunity to look about the room. The entire west wall was covered with maps—mostly old world maps that looked like they'd been salvaged from a classroom. They were overlapped to cover holes and tears making for some odd juxtapositions. Alaska and Ireland had become neighbors, while Australia now shared a border with Chile.

"Again?" Becton had turned his back to Clay and lowered his voice. "That's what you said last weekend... yeah, right... yeah, sure... I understand, I understand." He remained facing the wall for a second or two after hanging up the receiver. Then, turning back to Clay with a half-hearted smile, "Well, looks like I'm free for the weekend."

Clay smiled, "Yeah, I know how that goes." He was trying to remind himself that he could never call this man anything other than 'Bec'. He didn't dare slip and call him Billy as Sylvie had done.

"Well, I guess we could get started," Bec glanced at his watch. "Oh hell, let's break for lunch," he laughed.

Clay wondered if Bec's consistent good humor was just a front. Was he really that determinedly nonchalant or did he just not give a damn?

"I guess we could have a hamburger—or we could go out," Bec said inspecting the scanty contents of the refrigerator.

"You got any eggs in there?" Clay asked. "I can make an omelet."

"An omelet? Really?" Bec seemed genuinely interested.

"Yeah, sure. Let's see what else you've got in here," peering into the refrigerator Clay guessed that Bec ate a good many of his meals out. In his brief incarnation as a short order cook's apprentice a few years earlier Clay had learned enough to stand him in good stead. He gathered some sausage, cheese, a tomato, and rescued a green pepper on the brink of no return.

"Jeez, this is great," Bec said gratefully as he savored the first bite. "Really great—I get tired of hamburgers. Listen, if you want to cook up anything else just be my guest."

The two continued eating in silence. Clay was thankful the omelet had turned out so well.

"Maybe I should get a start on these if I'm going to have kitchen privileges," Clay said adding his empty plate to the pile of dirty dishes in the sink.

"No, no—save them for Michael—he'll probably be stopping by tonight."

"Michael?"

"Yeah, he's an old friend."

"You have a friend who likes doing dishes?"

"Well, it's not exactly that—you'll see," Bec smiled.

The rest of the afternoon was spent in what Bec called the writing room, a sort of makeshift office across the hall from Bec's living room. It contained only two desks and chairs and two long tables piled with notebooks and stacks of paper. The room was kept deliberately spartan, Bec told Clay, to keep distractions at a minimum. Clay wondered that the sound of the typewriter did not bother Bec, but he sat engrossed in his work—writing, thinking, rising occasionally to look through a notebook on one of the tables. Clay pecked away through several chapters. It was somewhat slow going due to Bec's handwriting and the way he squeezed afterthoughts in between the lines. The typewriter was an older electric model but it had a good, solid feel to it. The two men worked on in silence until nearly five o'clock.

Bec rose, stretched, and walked over to inspect the typewritten pages Clay had finished.

"Not bad...not bad at all for the first day," he pronounced. "So, what do you think of it?"

"Ah...very entertaining," Clay answered in mock seriousness. "You have some imagination," he looked at Bec and they both laughed.

Bec crossed back to the front window. "I've gotta get out of here for awhile," he said looking through the window toward the ocean. He turned suddenly seeming to have made up his mind. "I'm going out for awhile," he said moving across the room. "Oh, Clay," he stopped at the doorway, "do you know your way around town? I mean I guessed you're not from this area."

"You're right and no, I really don't know Trident Beach." Clay had long since stopped trying to conceal his southern accent, even finding it advantageous at times. Bec seemed to be reading his thoughts.

"I'll bet the ladies love that accent. Anyway, this time of year the best place in town for dinner is Braeden's—center of town, 8th Street—open year 'round—you can't miss it—just ask anyone. Okay—so, I'll see you later," Bec smiled and turned toward the hallway.

Clay nodded and rose from his chair. Straightening the stack of pages he had finished, Clay decided perhaps he needed to get out for awhile himself. As he started up the stairs for his room, he could hear Bec on the telephone through the open living room door.

"Michael...Yeah, it's me...No, she's not coming—so what else is new, right? You want to hit the Westside?... Yeah, okay—yeah, I guess we'd better—my car's not doing so well... Yeah, very funny—I'll see you in about half an hour."

Clay hurried quietly up the stairs and into his room. He was eager to get out and stretch his legs after sitting for so long but curiosity overcame him. He decided to wait the half-hour to try to catch a glimpse of this Michael. Clay finished unpacking, pausing every few minutes to look out the front windows. His patience was rewarded. At exactly five-thirty a sleek, silver Mercedes pulled up behind Clay's car. The sedan looked as if it had just been driven out of the showroom. 'Jesus!' Clay thought to himself—'this guy must do more than wash dishes'.

The man, about the same age as Bec, started toward the house. He appeared to be about Bec's height but with a much slighter build. Short, dark-brown, curly hair and glasses. He was dressed casually, but Clay could tell even from a distance—expensively. Bec met him halfway up the walk and the two stopped and talked for a moment before heading toward the car.

Clay grabbed his jacket and started down the stairs. He paused at the bottom, taking in the silence of the large, old house. The door to Bec's living room was wide open. Clay wondered again if this man just didn't give a damn—or perhaps he didn't have any secrets to protect. Clay rejected the idea of searching Bec's rooms for some proof that he was indeed Billy Becton. He was afraid of being discovered and also, he really did want to get some fresh air and stretch his legs. He felt a need to see the ocean and headed in that direction.

The water was calm and the beach deserted. Clay walked along the sand for several blocks before returning to Ocean Boulevard, the street closest to the beach. He knew the center of town was at least a mile away, but decided not to go back for his car. The walk felt good after the afternoon of sitting at the typewriter.

As Bec had said, Clay found Braeden's centrally located at the corner of Columbus and 8th Streets—just a block back from the beach. The food was good, nothing fancy, but good and cheaper than Clay had expected. He felt comfortable. It was the kind of a place where he didn't mind eating alone.

Clay thought about exploring the center of town after dinner but now, standing on the sidewalk outside Braeden's in the growing twilight he felt suddenly tired. He decided to postpone the sightseeing for another day and save his strength for the walk back to Bec's.

The air grew cool quickly after sundown. Clay could feel the chill through his thin summer-weight jacket. He reached the block Bec's house was on, but instead of continuing down the street, he turned and walked the two blocks to the beach. He was cold and tired but he wanted to see the ocean again—some need he didn't try to reason out. Just a desire to see it—to make sure it was still there perhaps—before he went to bed.

The wind was stronger but strangely more bearable as he approached the water. Now in the near-night the sound of the waves was everywhere. The darkness seemed to muffle their roaring, elongating the crisp crashes of day into furry echoes that sounded all around him. The sea had always held a fascination for Clay. Its hypnotic mystery terrified yet held him fast. As a young boy during infrequent family visits to the beach he had stood as in a trance for hours gazing at the vast, dazzling blue. He remembered that each time just as he had begun to feel more comfortable—that there might be a chance of establishing some sort of rapport with the ever-shifting waves—it had been time to return home.

Clay didn't know how long he had been standing lost to thought and reverie facing the sea, but the sky and the water were quite black now and he had a sense that they had been so for some time. Walking back toward Bec's house he checked his watch by the dim glow of a streetlight. Clay met no one on his way from the beach to the house. A few lights in each block indicated the year-round residents and autumnal weekenders.

The house was quiet. Apparently Bec was still out with his friend Michael. Clay had as yet seen nothing of Mr. Suey, the inhabitant of No. 6. It gave him a strange feeling being in the big, quiet house all alone. Perhaps it was simply that he didn't know the place that well or perhaps it was the absolute stillness. Clay stopped at the bottom of the stairs listening. No sounds of traffic, no wind, nothing. Weren't old houses supposed to creak or settle or something? Nothing—absolute quiet. Feeling uneasy Clay hurried up the stairs and into his room. Maybe the house knew why he was really there. He locked the door behind himself. He felt more comfortable now, but God, he was tired, drained. How long could he maintain the effort of this front as Bec's new typist? How long would he have to? Thank God this room had its own bathroom. It was tiny—probably a converted closet—but at least he didn't have to leave his room to use it.

The springs in the old mattress sang out a greeting as he settled onto the bed. A little soft, but not bad. He thought about the things his mother had always said concerning mattresses in public places and about the can of spray disinfectant she had carried with them on every family vacation. He laughed aloud remembering the way his father had always groused about having to wait for his mother to spray the bed thoroughly before he could lie down. Clay was tired, but it really wasn't all that late and he decided to read for awhile.

He jerked awake. It must have been the noise of his book falling to the floor. He turned away from the light. It seemed he had been dreaming—of the ocean...and of Sylvie? Yes, he had the feeling she had been there but he couldn't remember the details, just a vague sense of nearness to her. He had almost drifted back into sleep when he heard a dull thud, and then another. The sounds seemed to have come from the street. Clay rolled over, turned off the lamp, and walked through the dark room toward the front windows. The silver Mercedes shone dimly reflecting the weak light of the street lamp. Two dark figures huddled together moved slowly up the walk. Clay squinted trying to make his sleepy eyes work in the dim light. One of the people looked like Bec, but the other—perhaps a woman? The Mercedes took off. Well, Clay guessed the other person wasn't Michael at any rate.

He could hear them moving around in the living room below him. He opened the door to his room just enough to stick his head out into the dimly-lighted hallway. The muffled sounds of music and a woman's laughter came to him. Bec must have closed the living room door at that point. Clay closed and relocked his door. He moved quietly across the room. The music seemed to be loudest by the south wall. Clay carefully opened the large, round window. Bec must have had the window below open and the music climbed on the cool, damp air. The song was old, probably late sixties. It seemed familiar but Clay couldn't quite place it. His mind played over the melody as he strained for any bits of conversation. Van Morrison—yes, he was sure, but still he couldn't name the song. He could hear the low drone of their voices, Bec and the woman, but he couldn't make out what they were saying. Clay's neck ached under the strain of trying to hear and he was beginning to shiver against the cool, moist air filling his room. Latching the window quietly he made his way back to the bed. The street lamp cast a comforting soft light through the front windows. Clay checked his watch—twelve-thirty. The hell with getting undressed he thought as he slid onto the bed trying to make as little noise as possible. He was too tired to think any more tonight—about Bec, his female guest, or about Sylvie.

CHAPTER VI

Clay awoke in the classic 'I'm a little teapot' posture. The hand he'd been lying on was asleep. He tried to shake out the tingly feeling as he rose from the bed. Ten o'clock? God, he couldn't remember when he'd slept that late. The room was a blaze of pure yellow light. The sun promised another perfect day. He desperately hoped Bec had some coffee in that jumbled kitchen of his.

Halfway down the stairs it occurred to Clay that he might be intruding on Bec and his lady visitor. He paused for a second. The house seemed quiet. His need for a cup of coffee overcame any sense of propriety about disturbing his new employer.

Entering the kitchen through the hallway door at the back of the house, Clay was surprised to find Bec seated alone at the kitchen table reading a newspaper.

"Thank God!" Clay said, his eyes locking on the coffee pot on the counter. "Do you mind?"

"No, please—help yourself," Bec folded the newspaper and laid it aside. "Hey, were you afraid we might have a fire drill in the middle of the night?" he smiled indicating Clay's wrinkled clothes.

"Oh—right, I guess I'm a little out of it," Clay laughed, realizing he was still wearing the clothes he had fallen asleep in last night. "Ah, that's better," he murmured taking small sips of the hot coffee. "Sorry I slept so late—I mean I didn't know if you wanted me to do any typing today."

"Well, usually I don't believe in working on weekends, but if you wouldn't mind putting in a few hours today. It's been awhile since my last typist fled and things have gotten kind of backed up. Okay?"

"Sure, that's fine."

"There's some cornflakes if you're hungry," Bec said picking up the newspaper again.

"Thanks, but I don't think I'm ready for that yet," Clay replied, starting on his second cup of coffee. "Maybe I'd better get cleaned up before I start typing."

"Sure. I'll put the chapters by the typewriter for you. I may be going out for awhile."

Clay finished dressing and glanced out one of the east windows. The green Fiat was gone. No one seemed to be stirring downstairs as he opened the door to the writing room. Clay looked over the pages to be typed. 'Jeez, I wonder if he does his own research,' Clay thought. Then he remembered the night before. Had there really been a woman here with Bec or had he just dreamed the whole thing? He couldn't explain why, perhaps it was the laughter he had overhead, but he had an irrational feeling that she was a blonde.

Clay typed for awhile. The rest of the house still seemed empty. Carefully he took the photo Sylvie had given him from his wallet. He compared the handwriting on the back of the picture with Bec's cramped scrawl on the page he was typing. They were definitely similar but he was no handwriting expert. He just couldn't be sure. Turning the photograph over, Clay studied the picture for a moment. From it he could only draw the same conclusion as with the handwriting—similarities, but nothing certain.

Even with just a short break for lunch, the typing took Clay longer than he had expected. By the time he finished it was after six. Bec had still not returned home when Clay left the house and headed toward the beach. He realized this was the first time he'd been out all day. The ocean seemed very calm, almost unnaturally calm to Clay. Small ripples broke weakly into thick foam on the sand. The rest looked like dark jelly stretching to the horizon in the growing gray air. Clay envied the people who had lived here long and knew all the moods of the sea. He felt suddenly like a tourist...a voyeur to some great happening he couldn't comprehend and he turned back to the street.

Clay ate dinner again at Braeden's. It was more crowded than the night before. He guessed the nice weather had brought more weekenders to the shore. But the place still had a good feeling to it and the walk there and back did him good after the hours at the typewriter. Walking back alone through the dark streets, Sylvie was with him. She seemed to be taking over a growing part of his mind.

Clay was brought from his thoughts as he rounded the corner of Bec's block. Several vehicles lined the street. All the houses on the block were dark except for Bec's.

Clay thought of escaping to the beach—he wasn't much for crowd scenes. Maybe the cars belonged to people renting rooms? He couldn't quite convince himself of that but decided he might as well plunge in. Walking slowly, Clay took note of the vehicles. Besides his own car and Bec's Fiat there were Michael's Mercedes, a red mini-pickup truck, and a dark blue Chevy not more than a couple years old. On the opposite side of the street were four fairly late model cars of various makes and colors. 'Jeez,' thought Clay, 'I hope this guy's parties aren't quite as bizarre as his books.'

Clay opened the front door slowly. He was swallowed immediately by a wave of smoke, music, and voices—lots of voices talking and laughing. He was debating whether to brave the crowd spilling from Bec's living room into the hallway or simply retreat up the stairs to his room. He was saved from making a decision, however, as the front door opened behind him nearly knocking him over.

"Hey, Clay, you're just in time!" Bec shouted over the noise. He had his arm around a short, dark-haired girl with a sweet, round face. The other hand held a bottle of beer. From the look of their hair and their flushed faces Clay guessed they had been walking on the beach.

"This is Marianne," Bec shouted again into Clay's ear. "Come on, let me introduce you to everybody—at least the ones I know," he laughed.

Clay followed Bec and Marianne through the crowded hallway into an even more tightly-packed living room. A heavy, gray-white cloud hung over the room, but Clay noticed as they moved through, it seemed to be uniformly cigarette smoke. They moved slowly through the crowd, Bec shouting to be heard, Clay catching only about half the names flung at him as Bec made introductions. By the time they had made their way to the kitchen it was all just a blur of noise, smoke, and smiling faces. At least the kitchen was not quite as crowded and with the windows wide open the air was a little cooler if not much fresher. Bec opened the refrigerator. Clay wondered if this were the real reason it was normally almost empty. Every available space was filled with bottles and cans of beer. Bec handed Clay a bottle and got a fresh one for Marianne and himself. The light in the kitchen was much brighter affording Clay a better look at Marianne. She was definitely not the same woman he had seen coming up the walk with Bec the night before. She was much too short for that. His first impression had been that she was slightly chubby but now in the light he could see that it had only been an impression fostered by the roundness of her face and not supported by the rest of her body. She was short but very well-proportioned, petite, he guessed might be the proper term. Shiny, black hair in tight ringlets fell to her shoulders, framing her face. Her eyes were large and dark, but her most prominent feature was the cherubic smile that formed small dimples in her full cheeks. Clay couldn't help but smile back at her. She tried to engage him in small talk—about his new job as typist, about Bec's books while Bec talked with some of his other guests. They were just the usual first meeting, party-chatter type questions but Clay sensed they were motivated by a sincere desire to put him at ease and he appreciated her efforts.

After thirty or forty minutes Clay had had enough of the smoke and noise and excused himself knowing he would never be missed in the confusion. It took him awhile to work his way to the bottom of the stairs. Although the party was confined to the first floor, the noise it generated was everywhere in the old house. Clay's room, directly over the epicenter, was unbearable. The din from below seemed to reverberate and amplify as it spiraled upward through the building. Grabbing a heavy sweater Clay hurried back down the stairs and out the front door.

Freedom! He ran the two blocks to the beach trying to shake the stale smell from his hair and clothes. God, it felt good to get away from all those people. The wind was still light and a soft, black mist melded water and sky into one huge, incomprehensible whole. Between the fuzzy darkness and the intermittent breeze playing tricks on his ears, Clay could not tell just where the waves were breaking until he was almost on top of them. Several times he had to back step quickly to avoid being soaked.

Finding a soft place free of sand spurs on the sea side of a small dune Clay sat down facing the water. Hugging his knees to his bowed head he let the wind play over the back of his neck. The darkness around him was so intense it was hard to distinguish between keeping his eyes open and letting them close. He thought about Sylvie, letting her into his mind like a special treasure to be brought out and cherished in moments of solitary reverie. He wondered about her feelings for Becton, wondered if she were married, wondered a hundred things about her.

He didn't think he'd really fallen asleep, but Clay knew he had been sitting curled up lost in speculation and fantasy for a good while. His arms and legs ached as he tried to unfold them. Brushing the sand from his clothing he rolled his head around several times trying to loosen the muscles in his neck. Even holding his watch right up to his face, Clay could not make out the time in the thick darkness. He really didn't feel ready to return to the house, fearing the party would probably be running late. Turning up the collar of his shirt and shoving his hands into his pockets he started off southward down the beach. As he walked, Sylvie entered his thoughts again, but this time seemingly of her own volition.

Clay lost track of time and distance. Realizing he didn't know how far down the beach he had come he knew there would be no way of telling in this darkness how far back to walk. Turning away from the water, he decided the best course would be to head back toward Ocean Boulevard. The beach here was much wider than in Bec's neighborhood and for a few moments he wondered if he had somehow gotten turned in the wrong direction. Eventually he made out the hazy glow of a streetlight. The mist had gotten thicker—at least it appeared so, now away from the water. Clay was completely unfamiliar with this part of Trident Beach. The houses looked like those all up and down the beach, but there seemed to be many more vacant here than in the areas closer to the center of town. The rolling mist and dark shadowy beach houses gave an eerie feeling to the street, but he figured if he kept walking in this direction he'd have to run into Bec's neighborhood eventually. He nearly jumped when a motorcycle suddenly roared by on Columbus, the next street over. After walking for what seemed at least four times the distance he had covered on the beach, Clay finally reached Twenty-eighth Street and walked the two blocks west to Meridien Avenue and Bec's house. He was surprised to see that only Bec's car and his own remained in front of the house. Checking his watch, Clay was shocked to find that it was after three. The front door was still unlocked. Clay closed and locked it quietly behind him. The living room and hallway were the predictable disaster areas but the house was peaceful now. Clay climbed the stairs slowly, feeling the fatigue in his legs. Undressing quickly, he fell onto the bed greeted by the noisy springs.

CHAPTER VII

Clay awoke to early sun streaming through the front windows. He felt surprisingly refreshed for having slept only a few hours. After showering and dressing quickly he headed down the stairs. The house was quiet. Figuring Bec must still be asleep, Clay decided to have breakfast out and not chance disturbing him. Besides, for all he knew, the girl he had met last night, Marianne, might still be here. Closing the front door gently, Clay headed down the walk. He would help Bec clean up the mess from the party when he got back.

Borrowing an old bicycle he found at the house, Clay decided to cruise around and find some place to eat breakfast. It was a short trip. Halfway between Bec's and the center of town at the corner of Astor Avenue and Thirteenth Street he was attracted to a small Italian bakery by a sign promising hot coffee. As he entered the little shop he was pleasantly overpowered by the aroma of fresh baked goods and brewing coffee. Taking his mug and pastry, Clay chose a table by the window. The coffee was unusually good. He lingered over a third cup watching the steam from it form phantom wisps in the sunlight. He enjoyed the sun through the glass and felt warmed inside and out as he looked lazily over a newspaper left on the next table. Clay had the place almost to himself. The shop seemed to do a brisk business, but most of it was in take-out orders. Only one other table was occupied by an older man in a tweed sport coat working his way through the Sunday Times. The silence was broken only by the distant, muffled clatter in the kitchen and the occasional ring of the cash register as people came in to pick up orders. Clay hated to leave this warm nook, but the coffee was gone and he didn't really want a fourth cup.

The air outside was cool and it quickly brought Clay from the cozy lethargy of the bakery. Being still early, he decided to explore Trident Beach. Taking one of the main roads, Columbus Street, he cycled slowly through the middle of town past the small Sunday crowds brought out by the good weather. It was an old town, long-established. At its center were the squat two- and three-story brick buildings—the nucleus—flanked by the predominantly frame beach houses stretching to the north and south ends of town. Surprisingly even the few larger multi-storied hotels on the boardwalk just south of the town's center did not seem out of place. It all blended into a coherent whole—Trident Beach. Clay took note of the faded white seagulls painted on the long boardwalk which served as divider between town and beach. Bec had told him they were meant to keep real gulls from dropping clam shells on the boardwalk fearing they would be stolen by the painted birds.

Several gift stores and snack shops were open on the streets nearest the beach. Clay made mental notes as he rode, criss-crossing back and forth from the boardwalk to the inland side of town. Places for future excursions: an old movie theater, a small grocery store, used book shop, laundromat, library. He continued working his way northward until Columbus Street separated into three distinct streets. To the right, east, lay the beach and Surf Road. The road straight ahead, Essex, led to the next town up the coast. Clay took the left branch, Woodbine Drive, away from the ocean. The road narrowed and became a long, slow semi-circle rounding toward the southwest. Clay investigated several of the small side streets along the way. It was a fairly large area, a very pleasant residential neighborhood. Most of the houses had the look of year-round residences. This whole part of town had a different feel to it, almost out of place for being so close to the ocean. Perhaps it was the well-tended gardens and carefully coaxed lawns that gave it the look of a neighborhood pretending to be much farther inland. Only some of the street names gave it away: Dune Trail, Atlantic Road, Frigate Way. Clay put it in the back of his mind as a good place to take long walks in the future—that was providing he had a future here.

Clay was glad he had chosen to come out on the bicycle this morning. The peddling was easy on the uniformly flat streets. He found it the perfect way to explore the various parts of this long, narrow town. Clay turned southward again toward the center of town. This time, instead of riding down Columbus Street, he chose the alley directly behind it.

Clay was amazed at what he found there. The alleyway behind the central street stretched away before him for block after block. The concrete bottom curved up slightly at each side. Clay guessed this was designed for drainage and though it made bicycling a bit of a challenge, it was worth it. It was like discovering a whole secret world behind the buildings' facades. The alley was lined by the brick backs of stores and restaurants and the tall wooden fences of tiny backyards. Here and there a tree sent its branches in an arc over the way. In all it had a very closed-in, contained feeling to it like peering through a long tunnel. Clay pedaled slowly taking it all in: the smells—cooking and garbage, the barking dogs, the snippets of conversations overheard. He kept on until the alley's end at Tenth Street some distance from the town's center.

Continuing south, Clay came to the broad, flat, open beaches that characterized that end of Trident Beach. Here nothing stood between road and ocean but the yellow sand. That was what had struck Clay first about these South Jersey beaches—their color. He had been accustomed to the silkier gray sand of the North Carolina coast. At first sight, the coarse, yellow sand here had reminded him of yellow cornmeal. These beaches at the south end of town were favored by surfers whom Clay discovered to be a cliquish bunch—standoffish and a bit surly toward the uninitiated. His sightseeing appetite sated for the moment, Clay turned the bicycle toward Bec's.

The street in front of the house looked like a replay of the night before. Bec's Fiat was joined by Michael's Mercedes, the red pick-up, and the blue Chevrolet. 'Another party?' wondered Clay. His first instinct was to ride on past the house—somewhere—he didn't know where. But he knew he couldn't keep avoiding Bec's friends. They might be a valuable key in finding out more about Bec and besides, if he were going to be living and working in Bec's house he would have to get to know them eventually.

Clay walked the bicycle slowly toward the house, paused before the open front door and drew in a deep breath. To his surprise, the hallway and living room were completely free of litter. No signs remained of last night's party.

"Amazing isn't it?" Bec answered Clay's puzzled look. "Michael's magic fingers." Bec motioned Clay into the living room. "Hey, you want a beer?" Clay shook his head. "You remember Arnie Pridgen and Pete Tyndall from last night?"

"Yeah, how ya doin'?" Clay responded to their nodded greetings. He had only a blurred memory of the two faces in last night's crowd.

"And of course, Michael in the kitchen—Michael Kendrick."

Michael, busy at the kitchen sink, turned just long enough to give Clay a sidelong glance and an off-hand wave.

"You were up and out early this morning, Clay," Bec said resuming his place in one of the old armchairs on the far side of the room.

"Yeah, I thought I'd see some more of town—and I found a good place for breakfast—an Italian bakery on Astor Avenue."

"Mauro's—yeah, it's great—Marianne's uncle runs the place."

"Where are you from?" Arnie abruptly threw the question at Clay.

"North Carolina."

Arnie just grunted and puffed away on his cigarette.

"Don't mind Arnie, he gives everybody a hard time," Bec laughed.

Pete nodded in agreement. Arnie was just on the point of an expletive comeback when the phone rang. Bec leaned over from his chair to grab the receiver.

'Great!' thought Clay. 'Now I'll have to talk to these guys without Bec to run interference.' But he was spared this time.

"Pete, it's for you—Polly."

"What does perfect Polly want now, Petey?" mocked Arnie.

Pete brushed past Arnie to the phone.

"Polly is Pete's wife," Bec explained as Pete took the receiver.

The conversation was very brief, consisting mostly of Pete's nodding his head and murmuring, "uh-huh".

"I've got to split. Polly wants me to pick up something at her sister's in Cape May."

"Whipped!" muttered Arnie.

Pete crossed back to the other side of the room, giving Arnie the finger as he went.

"Pete, why don't you take Clay with you—give him the grand tour," Bec called across the room.

"Sure, you're welcome to come," Pete nodded toward Clay, seeming not to mind having a complete stranger foisted off on him.

The blue Chevrolet turned out to be Pete's. It was a perfect day for the ride south—sunny, the air just cool enough to make riding comfortable. Clay's main concern was what he could find to say to this Pete Tyndall. He knew he had to be on guard about what he revealed of himself. As the drive progressed, Clay found he needn't have worried. While Pete had seemed somewhat diffident in the company of his friends, he opened up into a veritable chatterbox with an audience of one, a stranger at that.

Clay found he had to do little more than nod or answer an occasional brief question to keep the conversation going. Pete seemed more than willing to give away information about Bec and his friends. Clay tried to be casual, watching the parade of beaches and small shore towns as they headed south. He felt like laughing out loud—he couldn't believe his luck. He knew that the details Pete was so freely supplying would have been very difficult to come by otherwise.

Clay longed for a notebook or tape recorder, but did his best to mentally store all the data that Pete poured out to him. He learned that Bec, Michael, Arnie, and Pete had met and become friends at Morgan College. Bec and Michael had been roommates. They all remained in touch after college, which according to Pete, Bec and Arnie had barely made it through. Bec had drifted around for awhile, married, divorced, and eventually fallen into writing his lurid novels. Michael had gone to study art in Paris where his mother lived. Judging from his car, clothes, and what Pete said, Clay gathered that Michael came from a very wealthy family. Pete and Arnie had been drafted and sent to Vietnam. Pete came back, married his high school sweetheart, and settled in the town where he had been born, Trident Beach. Now he shared an interest in his father's local exterminating service. Arnie had worked at a series of jobs up and down the coast, married, divorced, and married again.

The four had spent a lot of time at the Jersey shore while in college—weekends, summers. Most of the time it was Trident Beach, Pete's hometown, as they could always count on a free meal at Pete's house. One by one they had gravitated back to Trident Beach in the late seventies and early eighties. First Arnie, then Bec when his mother bought the house on Meridien Avenue, and finally Michael.

Clay enjoyed the drive. He was grateful that Pete had chosen the shore road instead of the Garden State Parkway, faster but farther inland. Apart from Pete's invaluable narrative, it gave Clay a chance to see more of the area. He had hoped to see something of Cape May, but Pete's sister-in-law lived on the northern fringes of town. After a quick stop to pick up a sewing pattern for Polly they were headed back to Trident Beach. Clay gathered there was no love lost between Pete and his wife's sister.

Pete filled the ride back with stories of their days at Morgan College. The expected anecdotes of rebellion and drunken pranks, usually with Arnie and Bec as the major perpetrators. By the time they pulled up in front of Bec's house, Clay felt he had known them all for quite some time. Perhaps his new-found knowledge would help him feel less uneasy in the company of Bec's friends. Still, when he and Pete found the house empty, Clay was relieved.

Checking his watch, Pete decided he'd better be off, too—Polly would be waiting for her pattern. Clay was alone in the big, empty house again.

CHAPTER VIII

It was another beautiful September day. High, feathery cirrus clouds arced against the blue sky. Mares' tails Clay's father had always called them. Clay had made good time on the drive from Trident Beach to Philadelphia. Arriving much earlier than he needed to, he walked through the streets surrounding Mallary's Restaurant, trying to shake off his nervousness. Clay knew he wanted to see Sylvie again. He had been looking forward to this meeting since last week, but why? There were so many questions. How could he hope to build let alone sustain a relationship based on these brief meetings? How could he get to see more of her? What did he really want from her anyway? Clay wasn't sure, he only knew he had to see her again, then maybe the rest would work itself out. He had wriggled out of typing for Bec on this Wednesday, promising to make up for it by working on Saturday. Pleading an important appointment in Philadelphia, Bec had let him go, joking that it was probably a rendezvous with a married woman. Clay laughed it off but during the drive and now walking toward the restaurant the words echoed in his mind, 'married woman'. Was she? He wasn't sure he wanted to know.

This time Clay had made a reservation, asking for a table at the back, against the wall. Sylvie arrived just a few minutes after he had been seated. He had half-expected her not to show up, but there she was following the hostess to his table. Clay jumped up to seat her. He felt like a squirrel had been let loose in his chest.

There was a flush to her face and slight ruffle in the dark hair that suggested Sylvie had hurried to make this meeting. Clay glimpsed a dark skirt and dark stockings as she slid into the chair opposite him. She was wearing a fuzzy sweater the color of burnt-orange autumn leaves. Clay wondered if there were any color she didn't look good in. The sweater's chunky, rolled collar set off her face, making her appear more fragile and child-like than ever.

"How have you been?" he asked.

"Oh, fine—just fine," she answered automatically, smiling.

Clay knew what she was waiting to hear.

"I think I've found him," he said.

"Really?" Sylvie tried to cover her delight but the corners of her mouth gave her away. "Where? Where is he?" she whispered her eyes gleaming.

"Now, I'm not positive it's him. Did Billy have any brothers or cousins around the same age?"

"Well...yes, he did have a brother a couple years older. Why?"

"I've found a guy living in Trident Beach going by the name Becton Delacroix. He could be the one in that picture you gave me, but I'm not sure yet."

Sylvie still looked hopeful, "But you can find out can't you? Tell me about him, please."

Clay outlined the last week for Sylvie. He watched her eyes widen with each detail.

"You mean you're actually living in the same house with him?" she broke in.

"Now, remember, I'm not positive he is Billy Becton."

Sylvie nodded and asked him to continue.

Clay went on, giving her an abridged version of Pete's account of their college days.

Sylvie looked thoughtful for a moment, "I think Billy did have a friend named Michael, but I'm not sure about the others."

They finished eating, Clay thankful he hadn't dropped any of his lunch in his lap, his attention had been focused so intently on Sylvie and her reactions to his report.

"I really have to go," she said checking her watch. "Can we meet here again next week? I mean, would that be convenient for you?" she asked hopefully.

"Yes, that will be fine. Maybe I'll have a definite answer for you by then," Clay told her. 'Convenient?' he thought. He had no idea where he'd be by next Wednesday, but he'd get to Mallary's somehow to see her.

As at their last meeting, Clay was tempted to follow Sylvie, to see where she went when she left the restaurant. But he checked himself, sat back down, and ordered another cup of coffee. He thought about her, about the soft, orange sweater he had wanted to reach out and touch. He had been so intent on studying her eyes and face that he had forgotten about the ring. He noticed it again as she handed him the envelope. The envelope. He had felt his throat tighten as he took it from her. At least he had gotten a better look at the ring this time. It didn't look like a wedding ring, but why did she wear it on that finger? Was it a wedding ring? Clay wanted to believe it wasn't.

Clay took his time driving back to Trident Beach. Clinging to the slow lane of the Atlantic City Expressway he savored the late afternoon sun and his memory of Sylvie. Reaching Trident Beach, Clay decided not to go directly back to Bec's. He drove to the nearly deserted south end of town, parked, and walked over the broad beach to the water's edge. He stood for some time arms folded, staring out at the ocean thinking about Sylvie, about Bec and what the next week might bring.

Clay looked overhead. The wind had widened a long vapor trail and now it resembled a giant dinosaur skeleton stretching across the sky. It had been great to see Sylvie again but it felt good to be back in Trident Beach, Clay thought as he turned his back to the sea.

Clay treated himself to a leisurely dinner at Braeden's before returning to Bec's house. 'Jesus,' he thought as he parked his car behind those of Michael, Arnie, and Pete. He wondered if he'd ever feel comfortable with Bec's friends. He opened the front door slowly. Music was coming through the open door to Bec's living room. Steely Dan.

"Come on, come on," Arnie's voice sounded above the others.

Clay hesitantly poked his head in the doorway. "How y'all doin'?"

Pete smiled, Michael nodded, Arnie looked annoyed.

"Was your mission to Philly a success?" Bec asked.

"Yeah, it was okay," Clay answered, not wanting to volunteer anything more.

"Come on, let's go," Arnie cut in impatiently.

"We're going to the Westside. It's a bar on the other side of town." Bec nodded toward Clay. "You want to come along?"

"Thanks, maybe another time." Clay had visions of a smoke-filled hole-in-the-wall populated by local regulars. He really didn't feel up to that tonight and he guessed from Michael's and Arnie's grim looks that they weren't overjoyed at the prospect of his joining them. Bec grabbed a jacket and followed Michael and Arnie to the front door.

"You coming, Pete?"

"Nah, I'd better get home."

Arnie rolled his eyes. "Whipped," he mumbled as he headed down the walk.

Alone again in the great, old house, Clay hurried upstairs to his room. Even now he couldn't bring himself to go through Bec's things. He would have to find another way of determining if he was indeed Billy Becton.

Clay realized he'd fallen asleep reading when he was awakened by the low bass throbs of Bec's stereo coming through the floor from below. Clay strained to make out the melody—Van Morrison, again. He couldn't hear any voices. The only cars on the street were his own and Bec's. Clay wondered drowsily if Bec had another female visitor, or the same one he had heard laugh before, or Marianne...as he drifted back to sleep.

CHAPTER IX

The next day brought dark, low clouds and a steady rain. The old house, somber and full of shadows, seemed to reflect the mood of the weather outside and the writer inside. Clay pecked busily away at the typewriter. Bec spent most of the morning scribbling silently in his notebooks—rising occasionally to shuffle about the room somnambulantly—checking to see if the rain had stopped. After lunch he disappeared to the back of the house for a long nap. Clay spent the rest of the day typing, deciphering Bec's handwriting, wondering how he had the nerve to write this stuff.

Around six o'clock the rain stopped and Clay and Bec went out to Terry's on Columbus Street, a small sandwich shop a few blocks from the house. Bec talked about some ideas he had for a new book.

"Something a little different, you know, like 'Sex Slaves of Saturn.'"

In response to Clay's pained expression Bec added, "never underestimate the power of alliteration."

"Did you ever think of writing something else—I mean a different kind of writing?"

"Nah, I figure I might as well stick to what I'm good at—flesh in hot lather," Bec laughed.

"Now that'd make a good title for you."

"Too late—I already used it on my second book."

When they got back to the house, they found Arnie's red pick-up out front and Arnie in the living room. He was sprawled in an armchair in front of the television, beer in one hand, a cigarette in the other. He scowled as the two entered.

"I know that look," Bec said. "You've had another fight with Grace?--(his wife)," he added in an aside to Clay.

"Yeah, so what else is new?" Arnie replied sourly. Clay wondered, 'does this guy ever smile?'

"Anything on?" Bec asked glancing at the television. Before Arnie could answer the front door opened.

"Well, I see the gang's all here," Michael said stepping into the living room. As before he was impeccably dressed in expensive, casual clothing. Michael appeared to Clay to be as naturally suited to this attire as Arnie was to his well-worn sweatshirt and jeans.

"Who wants to go to the Westside and check out the chicks?" Arnie asked stretching as he rose to his feet.

"Another fall from Grace, Arnie?" Michael deadpanned.

"Not me," answered Bec, "I'm expecting a call from Lydia tonight."

Arnie shook his head.

"Sure, why not, let's go," Michael turned back toward the door. Clay remained silent, figuring the invitation didn't include him.

"So—you want to watch some TV?" Bec asked. Clay heard the Mercedes and the pick-up roar off down the street as he settled into the armchair Arnie had vacated.

About halfway through a mediocre cops-and-robbers movie the phone rang. Sensing that Bec might want some privacy, Clay excused himself to go upstairs. He paused for a moment outside the living room door, thought about eavesdropping on Bec's call but couldn't bring himself to do it. As he climbed the stairs, Clay caught fragments of Bec's side of the conversation... "So, are we on for this weekend?... Friday?...Saturday, then?...what time?..."

Clay woke up early to nearly blinding sun filling his room. Opening the large front window he let the cool, gusty wind hit him full in the face. Invigorated, he dressed quickly and left the still quiet house for a walk on the beach. 'God, why can't every day be like this?' he asked himself as he strode southward along the water's edge.

Returning to the house, Clay found Bec in the kitchen, in a mood to match the glorious weather.

"Sorry there's nothing but corn flakes," Bec said apologetically.

"That's okay," Clay instinctively went for the coffee pot.

"I always plan to try something different but when I get to the grocery store I get so overwhelmed I end up with corn flakes every time.

"Yeah, somebody ought to propose a treaty for the nonproliferation of breakfast cereals."

"Right," laughed Bec.

"Be all right if I use the kitchen tomorrow night?" Clay asked.

"Sure—planning a cozy dinner for two?"

"No, just thought I'd fix a steak and salad for my-self—something like that."

"Sure, I'll be leaving early tomorrow morning for New York City. You'll have the place to yourself."

"Thanks—New York?"

"Yeah, I'm going to see Lydia, this girl I know. She works up there." Bec looked serious for a moment, almost embarrassed. "Look man, I know I should have talked to you about this before, but this weekend since I'll be gone and everything—I mean, the thing is I'd appreciate it if you didn't do any drugs while you're here in the house. What you want to do outside's your own business—but I've been busted a couple times and the local cops keep a pretty close watch on the place. I mean, I can't afford to take any chances."

"Sure, that's cool—I understand."

Bec looked relieved. "Besides, my mother'd prob-ably kick me out of here," he laughed returning to his normal, carefree expression.

They spent the day in the writing room typing and scribbling. Bec's mood was much lighter than the day before, stopping occasionally to ask Clay's opinion on a turn of phrase, chuckling often to himself as he wrote. Clay couldn't tell if Bec's mood was in reaction to the weather or in anticipation of his trip to New York. At one point, Clay was surprised to see Bec jump up and dance around the room waving a thick spiral notebook in the air.

"A new notebook—clean, unused—virgin territory just waiting for my far-flung fantasies—I love it."

Around six o'clock Bec took off to join Michael at the Westside. Clay went for dinner and a movie in Concourse, a small town a few miles inland. When he got back at eleven, Clay was surprised to find that Bec's Fiat was already back and the only car in front of the house. The place was quiet and dark except for the dim hall light. Getting ready for an early start to New York in the morning Clay guessed.

When Clay awoke the next morning, Bec was already gone. The house seemed empty, almost forbidding without him. Clay thought about escaping to the beach, but he had promised Bec he would work this Saturday to make up for his absence last Wednesday. He spent the day typing, trying to keep his mind on the work before him. Several times he was tempted to steal back to Bec's bedroom and search for clues to his real identity but he had the uneasy feeling that one of Bec's friends might appear suddenly and catch him at it. 'Some private investigator!' he thought. He was relieved at the end of the day to be able to shake off the house and go for dinner at Sunset Pizza on Tenth Street near the boardwalk. The hell with cooking his own dinner. He couldn't hack that tonight alone in that house. Afterward, a long walk on the beach.

Clay really didn't want to return to the dark, empty house but the cold wind off the water was getting the better of him. He was surprised to see lights in the windows of Bec's living room. Arnie, Michael, Pete? Clay wondered but their cars were not on the street. Clay moved cautiously from the hall through the empty living room into the kitchen where the lights were also on. He breathed a sigh of relief when he saw Bec seated at the kitchen table, a half-eaten pizza in front of him.

"Jesus, I thought you were a burglar," Clay told him.

"Right—nothing worth stealing around here," Bec half-laughed.

"So, how come you're here? I thought..."

"Yeah, New York City. Well, best laid plans—right?" Bec seemed uncharacteristically melancholy. Clay thought perhaps it was the almost empty six-pack of beer on the table beside the pizza.

"You want some?" Bec pointed toward the pizza.

"No thanks, I had the same thing for supper."

"Have a beer then. There's some cold ones in the frig."

Clay helped himself to a beer and sat down at the kitchen table opposite Bec.

"What happened to your big dinner?" Bec asked. "I saw the steak and stuff still in the frig."

"I felt like getting out tonight after typing all day."

"Yeah, I looked over what you got done to-day—you're doing a great job."

"Thanks."

Bec looked suddenly sad. Clay guessed he was flirting with serious inebriation. "You okay?" he asked Bec who was now staring blankly at the pizza.

"Huh?"—oh, yeah—it's just I was really looking for-ward to this weekend—oh, well—screwed again. And then to top it all off, my car broke down."

Clay was afraid to press too far with his questions, hoping Bec would volunteer more, hoping the beer might loosen his tongue.

"So, how come you're the only one here tonight? Everybody at the Westside?"

"No, Michael and Arnie went over to Atlantic City."

"Atlantic City—I've only been through there a couple times—never really checked it out. All glitz and glamour?"

"Glitz and glamour," Bec echoed hollowly. "It's not what it used to be. All those bright lights and big, hard-edged new buildings. I mean I know the town had its problems and everything, but it used to be a place with a special feeling to it—that feeling's gone now."

Clay could see emotions breaking over Bec's face like waves, first sadness followed by joy as a happy recollection kindled itself in his mind.

"I used to know this guy," Bec continued, "this was years ago—before all the new buildings and shit. His summer job was to dress up in this giant peanut costume and go up and down the boardwalk handing out free samples. He said the costume was hotter than hell, pigeons were an occupational hazard, and he usually ended up frightening small children. Some job, huh?" Bec laughed at the memory of it.

Clay was afraid to interrupt while Bec was in this talkative mood, hoping he might reveal something useful. And besides in some strange way Clay found himself enjoying this reverie of Bec's.

"We used to go over there to Atlantic City sometimes on weekends when we were in school," Bec went on, "you know—just for something to do. Anyway, there used to be this place—a restaurant—dining room—in one of the big, old hotels. You could see it from the boardwalk. There was this tiny garden with a fountain separating it from the boardwalk." Bec gazed absently, remembering. "It always looked pretty fancy—you know—white linen table cloths, silver, crystal. I used to walk by and think maybe someday when I was older and had the money I'd get all dressed up and eat there—see what it was like on the inside looking out at the boardwalk. In a way I guess I thought that's what being really grown up was all about—sitting with a pretty lady in a place like that. Anyway, by the time I had enough money to give it a try—damn if they hadn't torn the whole thing down. Damn..."Bec trailed off.

From the expression on Bec's face, Clay knew he had to intervene before Bec slipped inexorably into the morose. He had to give the conversation a new turn.

"I see Michael's cleaned up the kitchen again," Clay nodded toward the sink, gleaming and free of dirty dishes.

"Oh, yeah, good old Michael," Bec smiled.

"Can I ask you something? I mean I know it's none of my business but is Michael a little, uh..." Clay shook his hand with mock gentility.

"Michael? Nah—you mean because he washes the dishes and everything? No, that's just something he's always done –says it helps him think. Who am I to argue—I hate cleaning—so it works out great."

"I just thought I'd better ask—just in case—so I didn't say something to offend him."

"No problem. Michael's cool. You ought to see him at the Westside. I've never known a guy to have such great luck with the ladies. Ladies..."

Clay sensed another slide toward the moribund and yanked the conversation in yet another direction.

"Were you in Vietnam?"

Bec looked surprised at the abrupt change of subject. "No, I lucked-out with my lottery number. Pete and Arnie were drafted though."

"My two older brothers went over—enlisted, can you believe that?"

"Insanity run in your family?"

"Possibly—I've always thought maybe I was adopted or left by aliens or something—don't really seem to fit in with the rest of the bunch." The last thing in the world Clay wanted to talk about was his family, but it seemed to be leading Bec away from a crying jag so he continued. "I've always thought of my two older brothers as 'the twins' even though they're two years apart—I guess because they're so much alike—and so different from me. My mother's the typical southern belle—built-in service for twelve and all that."

"Wonder what she'd have to say about your new job?" Bec laughed.

The first thing that flashed through Clay's mind was his brief stint in Uncle Bert's office, then he realized that of course Bec was talking about his job as typist of semi-pornographic literature.

"Yeah, she'd love that," Clay laughed, too, guessing his mother would probably have found both professions equally distasteful.

"Jeez, I'm really beat. I'm gonna hit the sack," Bec stood up suddenly, swaying slightly.

"Yeah, me too. See ya tomorrow." 'So much for pumping him for information,' Clay thought. 'Uncle Bert would really have a laugh at my abilities as a detective,' Clay smiled ruefully as he climbed the stairs to his room.

Clay was up and out early the next morning as it was Sunday and he guessed Bec's friends would be dropping by. Besides, why spend his day off in that house? He got in his car and began drifting south with no particular destination in mind. The early fog burned off into a brilliant, late-September day. Clay stopped frequently at different beaches on his way southward. Around one o'clock he stopped at Sea Isle City, bought a hot dog and sat down on the beach to eat it.

A flock of geese suddenly appeared in the sky overhead. The black and silver of their over- and under-wings alternating as if someone had thrown a handful of glittering confetti high into the air. Clay couldn't think of any place he would rather have been on that sunny day, except perhaps with Sylvie. Or to have Sylvie here with him—yes—that would make it perfect.

At late afternoon, Clay headed back toward Trident Beach. Not wanting to return to the house yet, he spent the rest of the day walking on the beach near the center of town. Once Clay thought he saw Bec from a distance with a tall, blonde girl but he couldn't be sure. As daylight faded, Clay left the water's edge for dinner at Braeden's. He had come to feel that any time spent with the ocean was never time wasted.

CHAPTER X

The next two days were gray and uneventful. The low clouds looked like long rows of cotton batting. Bec scribbled, Clay typed. When he fell into bed Tuesday night, Clay was still uncertain as to what he would tell Sylvie at their meeting the next day. As the week before, he had arranged with Bec to have Wednesday off for his drive to Philadelphia. Clay wished he had something definite to tell Sylvie. He wanted to know if Bec really were Billy Becton, and yet—what then? If he verified Bec's identity as Becton and told Sylvie? The search for Becton was Clay's only link to Sylvie. If it were broken would he be able to forge a new one to sustain the relationship? Besides, he was growing to like this new life in Trident Beach. Maybe he'd think of what to tell Sylvie tomorrow morning. Yes, Clay thought sleepily, perhaps morning would take care of it.

Morning did.

Clay showered and dressed leisurely. When he went downstairs for breakfast he found Bec leaning over the kitchen sink using a small mirror propped against the window sill to shave.

"Light in my bathroom burned out," Bec explained between strokes.

Clay poured himself a cup of coffee and turned toward the kitchen table. As he sat down something caught his eye. Bec was wearing a tank-type tee shirt revealing a small tattoo on his left shoulder. Even from across the room, Clay could tell it was a fleur-de-lis identical to the ones Billy Becton had used in signing his letters to Sylvie. Somehow Clay managed to get through the cup of coffee and escape to his car.

Most of the drive to Philadelphia was a blur. Clay had not planned to leave Trident Beach so early and arrived in the city with a couple hours to spare. He filled the time walking aimlessly around Center City thinking of what to say to Sylvie. In the end Clay knew he had no choice but to tell her the truth. He couldn't hide his discovery from her. He would simply have to hope that it wouldn't be their last meeting.

As usual, Clay arrived at Mallary's early. His table was ready so he sat down and began absently looking at the menu which he had long since memorized. His mind played over Sylvie's possible responses to the information he had for her. He was so absorbed she surprised him arriving exactly at two. Suddenly she was there again sitting across the table from him—close enough to touch.

They exchanged the usual pleasantries and ordered. Clay knew he couldn't put it off any longer.

"I've got some good news for you."

"Really?" her eyes sparkled.

Clay told her about the past week culminating in the discovery of the fleur-de-lis tattoo.

"I can't believe it—I mean I do believe it—it's just been such a long time—I was afraid..." Sylvie stopped to catch her breath.

"I guess the question now is how do you want to proceed?"

Sylvie looked surprised. Surely, Clay thought, she must have had some idea what she wanted to do if Becton were found.

"Well, I don't know," she began uncertainly, "can't we just go on with things the way they are?"

Clay was dumbstruck. This possibility had not occurred to him. Could they go on as before? He felt like taking Sylvie in his arms and whirling her around the room. Trying to keep his elation under control he asked, "you mean you want me to keep an eye on him and let you know what he's up to?"

"Oh, yes—I mean if you can do that."

"Sure, no problem."

"Oh, that's great," Sylvie beamed and repeated in a whisper as if to herself, "that's so great, you really found him."

As before, Sylvie had to rush off just before three-thirty. She rose, thanked Clay, and handed him the envelope full of cash all in one swoop before hurrying out.

Clay couldn't believe his good luck. He would be able to see her again. The glow of good fortune warmed him through a second cup of coffee at Mallary's and all during the drive back to the shore. Shunning the Atlantic City Expressway, Clay returned via a series of back roads, considering himself lucky to have gotten lost only twice. When he reached Trident Beach he was still so high he felt like dancing on the sand. He managed to confine himself to a brisk jog up and down the beach, trying to work off some of the giddiness before returning to Bec's. Out of breath, Clay walked slowly back the way he had come. Now back down to earth, he started asking himself questions. Why didn't Sylvie want to see Bec herself? Why did she still want someone to keep tabs on him? Better yet, why was she willing to pay someone to keep tabs on him? And lastly, what could he do to make her eyes sparkle the way they did at the mention of Billy Becton's name?

Clay stopped and picked up some groceries on his way back to Bec's at Reno's a little market on Strayport Road near the center of town and Mauro's bakery. Still in a great mood he didn't even mind the cars parked in front of the house—Michael's, Pete's, and a tan Toyota he hadn't seen before.

Steely Dan was playing to an empty living room. Clay walked down the hall toward the back of the house and into the kitchen where he found everyone gathered. It turned out the Toyota belonged to Marianne. Everyone was in good spirits, even Michael seemed lighter than usual.

"Whatcha got there?" Bec asked as Clay deposited the grocery bags on the kitchen counter.

"Just thought I'd pick up a few things. I can fix something if anybody's interested," Clay answered unloading the bags.

"I'm afraid I have to get home," Pete said heading for the door. "Thanks anyway. See you all later."

"Yeah, okay—what do you think?" Bec asked Marianne.

"Sure, sounds great," she smiled her sweet smile.

"Why not?" Michael said in a surprisingly congenial tone.

'My God,' thought Clay, 'everyone must be in a good mood on this great day.' Clay began busying himself with the meal. Bec and Michael got a beer from the refrigerator. Marianne had drifted into the living room and was shuffling through the albums by the stereo.

"You need any help? Not that we'd probably know what the hell to do," Bec laughed.

"Either of you guys know how to make a salad or some dressing?" Clay asked.

Bec and Michael shook their heads.

"How about Marianne?"

"Marianne make a salad?" Bec looked surprised. He and Michael exchanged glances and laughed.

"Marianne probably thinks Miracle Whip is some kind of S&M paraphernalia."

"I heard that, Michael!" Marianne shouted from the next room.

"You'll have to admit cooking isn't exactly your strong suit," he shouted back.

Clay had things well under way when Arnie joined the group. Clay wondered if even the sour apple might be in a good mood today.

"So, what's going on?" Bec asked Arnie as he reached for a beer.

"Not much—what's he up to?" Arnie nodded toward Clay.

"He's fixing dinner for us," Bec smiled.

"Too bad, I've already eaten."

"Don't tell me Grace has taken you back, again?" Michael chimed in.

"Yeah, what can I say?"

"Not much," Bec added, "she must be nuts."

"No lie," Arnie said sitting down at the kitchen table.

"It's beginning to smell pretty good, Clay," Bec was fishing around in one of the drawers for some silverware.

"Shouldn't be too much longer."

"You're not using any of that MSG stuff, are you?" Arnie asked abruptly. "I saw this thing on TV the other night about how it eats holes in your brain or something," he added seriously.

"Come on, Arnie, since when did you become an authority on chemical additives?" Michael jeered. "Weren't you the one who used to think that Spanish fly would cure the common cold?"

Arnie grumbled but didn't deny it.

Clay set up everything buffet-style on the kitchen table: tossed salad, Spanish rice, and rolls from Marianne's uncle's bakery. Everyone found chairs in the living room, balancing plates on their laps.

"This is great!" Bec managed between mouthfuls. Marianne nodded in agreement, smiling.

"Yeah, really not bad," Michael added.

"Thanks, glad you like it," Clay was just grateful he had picked up such a useful skill during his years of drifting from job to job.

"There hasn't been anybody around here who could cook since Jason moved to California," Bec said.

From the subsequent conversation Clay gathered that Jason was another college friend—somewhat out of favor for committing the unpardonable sin of moving to the West Coast. The mention of his name prompted several reminiscences of school days from Bec, Michael, and Arnie. Clay and Marianne listened and laughed. Clay found he enjoyed watching Marianne. Something about the play between her eyes and her mouth, as if one seemed always about to give the other away.

After dinner, Michael did the dishes and cleaned up the kitchen while the others watched television. Clay had to agree with Bec, it was nice to have someone around who enjoyed cleaning. About eleven, Michael and Arnie left. As Clay climbed the stairs to his room, he heard Marianne's soft laughter as the music changed to Eric Carmen.

Clay lay in bed, his arms folded behind his head, waiting for sleep to come. For a day that had started in near panic at the discovery of the fleur-de-lis tattoo, this had turned out to be one of the best days Clay could remember in some time. He had felt much more at ease with Bec and his friends—had even enjoyed listening to their stories. But most important of all, he would be able to see Sylvie again. Whatever happened, that would be enough to sustain him through the week to come.

Clay was awakened the next morning by the sound of the front door slamming. He looked out the window to see Marianne hurrying down the walk to her car. Downstairs Clay found Bec leaning over the sink.

"What the hell are you doing?" Clay laughed as Bec turned to face him.

"I just thought I'd try this stuff Marianne left here," he held up the can of mousse he was foaming onto his hair.

"Somehow I don't think it's the real you."

"Smells pretty good though doesn't it?"

"It smells like Marianne."

"Yeah, I guess you're right. Do you think there's any possibility this stuff causes brain damage?"

"Very possible," laughed Clay.

The two spent that day and the next writing and typing. Bec was in good spirits as he had another trip to New York planned for Saturday—last weekend's disappointment apparently forgotten.

The house was quiet without Bec. As before, Clay spent Saturday typing. The only visitor that weekend was Pete who stopped by on Sunday afternoon, unaware that Bec was away.

"Sorry I'm afraid I'm the only one here," Clay greeted Pete from a lawn chair on the front porch where he had been reading the Sunday paper. "Bec's in New York City."

"Oh, gone to see Lydia, again? I hope it works out better this time."

"Yeah, he was pretty bummed out last weekend. You want a beer?"

"Sure, why not?" Pete smiled.

Pete seemed in no hurry to leave. Clay guessed that this was his time away from the family to do as he pleased and he wasn't about to waste it whether Bec was home or not.

"Has Bec known Lydia a long time?" Clay asked hoping that Pete wouldn't find the question too nosy.

"Yeah, he's gone out with her off and on for quite awhile. She used to live here, but then she got a better job in New York. I think Bec wishes she were closer."

Clay's fears were unfounded. Not only didn't Pete mind answering his questions, he seemed genuinely appreciative of the chance to talk about Bec and his other friends. Of the four, Clay guessed that Pete was low man on the totem pole. As it turned out, he was a year behind the other three in school and so had missed out on the initial shenanigans. Now, his obligations to wife, children and parents kept him from spending as much time with his friends as he might have liked. Clay sensed that Pete enjoyed having someone around who was even less initiated than he into Bec's cadre—someone he could impress with his knowledge of Bec and the others and their exploits. Clay also recognized in Pete a familiar trait. Familiar perhaps because it was one he shared—the need to be liked or at least not to be disliked.

At the end of the afternoon they parted, both with a sense of satisfaction. Pete feeling important for a change. Clay thankful at having received information without having to ask a lot of questions. Pete had told story after story of Arnie's infidelities and drunken indiscretions, Michael's wealthy family, and Bec's romances—ricocheting between Lydia, Marianne and many others. Too many for Clay to remember all their names. He did notice, however, that Sylvie's name was never mentioned. Late that night, in his room reading, Clay was startled by a noise at the far end of the hall. He moved quietly to the door of his room and opened it slowly, just a crack. Knowing that Bec had not returned yet and he was alone in the house, Clay wasn't sure what to expect. Certainly not what appeared as he looked down the hall toward the back of the house. The overhead light at that end of the hall was burned out. In the dim light of the large hall window an indistinct white shape moved from one of the back rooms into the hallway.

'Jesus!' thought Clay. 'What now—ghosts?' Not that the old house wasn't dark and creepy enough to be haunted, he just wasn't quite ready to accept that. Clay stepped cautiously out into the hallway. Slowly the white shape approached him.

"Who are you?" Clay asked, relieved that the apparition had solidified under the light into an old man in a white nightshirt.

"Why, I'm Mr. Suey," he responded matter-of-factly as if Clay should have known. "Do I know you?"

"No, sir, my name is Clay Trinian. I'm staying in No. 1 and working for Bec."

"Ah, yes—I thought I heard a noise," Mr. Suey said moving toward the hall window at the front of the house. Clay joined him at the window just in time to see Bec coming up the walk.

"My, Mr. Becton's out late this evening isn't he?" the old man observed absently. "He really ought to do something about that old car of his. Is that your car...Mr. Trinian, the white one?" he asked motioning toward the street.

"Yes, sir, it is."

"Well, I'll just have to buy new cars for both of you. Yes, that's it −new cars for both of you!" he repeated definitively as he marched slowly back down the hall.

Clay alone again in the hallway couldn't swear that he hadn't been dreaming. He remembered Bec saying something about a Mr. Suey in No. 6—but new cars?

Bec was late getting to work the next morning. Clay had already been typing for a couple hours when Bec entered the writing room. His weekend had been a success—that was obvious—he was positively beaming. Bec no sooner sat down at his desk than Michael arrived. Clay was surprised never having seen him there on a weekday morning before.

"Just thought I'd drop this by—see what you think before I go any farther," Michael handed Bec a large sketch book.

"Yes, oh yes, I like it," Bec smiled approvingly.

"Any suggestions?"

"No, looks great. What do you think, Clay?" he turned the sketch toward Clay. Clay was struck, first by the quality of the sketch and then because it triggered the memory of last night's apparition. The sketch showed a woman in a filmy, white peignoir hurrying down a dark passageway. The white figure immediately reminded Clay of Mr. Suey cum nightshirt.

"Well? What do you think?" Bec repeated.

Clay realized he had been staring blankly at the picture. "Oh—it's great, really, Michael—I had no idea—it's just that it reminded me of something that happened last night." Clay still not sure if he had dreamed the whole thing, related the incident to them. Bec and Michael laughed.

"Sorry I forgot to tell you Mr. Suey was coming back from Florida," Bec apologized, "he's a trip isn't he?"

"Yeah—is he all right? I mean he kept talking about buying us new cars."

"Don't worry—he's always promising all sorts of things—he never follows through on any of it though." Bec replied. "Not that he couldn't—he's worth a bundle. He just never parts with any of it."

"He may be a little bit crazy but he's no fool," added Michael.

"He kind of surprised me last night coming out of the shadows like he did," Clay said.

"Yeah, our Mr. Suey's one of a kind," Bec smiled.

"You might say the generous Mr. Suey is sui generis," Michael interjected.

"Jeez, Michael," Bec groaned.

"Sorry, I just couldn't help myself. So, do you want me to go ahead and finish the sketch?"

"Yeah, it looks great," Bec replied. "I wish you'd agreed to do one of my cover illustrations before this."

"Better late than never," Michael said as he turned to leave.

Clay had been struck by the quality of Michael's sketch. Even in the brief look he had gotten he could tell that Michael was talented. Enough realism for a cover illustration, but his own style was definitely evident.

"I had no idea he was so good," Clay said after Michael had gone.

"Yeah, he does commercial art—advertisements, things like that. I keep telling him he ought to be doing something else—you know his own stuff."

"He doesn't?"

"No, he always says he's not interested—something about the rejection ethic."

"Hmm. So, which one of the books is Michael's sketch for?" Clay asked.

"'The Lady Says Maybe'," Bec replied. "That was the one that did in my last typist," he laughed.

CHAPTER XI

Wednesday, again. Clay waited until mid-morning to hit the Atlantic City Expressway toward Philadelphia. As always, the big steering wheel felt good in his hands—felt right. He had resisted all attempts by family and friends to trade the old '66 Fairlane in on a newer model. The car was ten years old when Clay took possession and twenty now. It had originally belonged to his parents. It had been passed down to each of his older brothers in turn then to Clay where it stopped when their younger sister got a brand new car for her sixteenth birthday. The Fairlane had become a trusted, old friend, one of the few constants in his life in the years since leaving home. It was more to him than a steel skin, pins, rings. The driver's seat knew his contours so well it was like slipping into a body-size glove—a living cocoon—humming, purring, barreling down the road. Toward Sylvie.

Clay's table wasn't quite ready when he reached the restaurant. He took the opportunity to check a city phone directory in the foyer. No listing for a Sylvie Daros—no Daros at all. Clay considered the possibilities—an unlisted phone number or perhaps she lived in one of the many suburbs surrounding the city or perhaps she hadn't given him her real name. Clay discounted the last idea almost immediately. He couldn't believe she would invent an alias like Daros. He couldn't imagine her first name being anything other than Sylvie—it seemed so much a part of her—or at any rate so much a part of his image of her.

Sylvie arrived just as the hostess was about to seat Clay. They made their way to the usual table at the back of the restaurant. Clay was aware of a faint, familiar scent as he followed Sylvie across the room. Hyacinths.

As at their prior meetings, Clay related the activities of the week before. The better Clay got to know Bec, the more uneasy he felt talking about him, revealing the details of his life to Sylvie. He felt as if he were betraying a friend but it was worth it to see her eyes light up. When three-thirty came, she handed him the envelope filled with cash as before. This time Clay handed it back to her unopened. He just couldn't keep taking her money.

"No, really, I'm there anyway and I'm getting paid for being his typist," Clay assured her.

"But can you do that—what about your other cases?"

"Oh, uh—my uncle's handling them. I'm taking a little time off from the business." Clay was glad that Sylvie didn't ask what he was getting out of their arrangement. He didn't want her money, the chance to see her again was enough. Perhaps she knew that.

This time when Sylvie left Clay was ready. Paying the check on the run, he kept back just far enough so that she would not see him. After leaving the restaurant she crossed the street, walked to the end of the block and turned the corner. Clay turned that corner just in time to see her enter a building in the middle of the block.

Clay hesitated then began walking slowly. After all, he could always feign coincidence if he ran into Sylvie this close to the restaurant. The sign over the doorway read 'Lady Anne's School of Dance'. Clay positioned himself strategically in a small bookstore across the street from the dancing school. He found a spot at the front of the shop where he could leaf through books while keeping an eye on the doorway across the street. Although it seemed an eternity, it was only a few moments before Sylvie reappeared—but she was not alone. A little girl in a raincoat over pink leotard and tights trotted energetically at Sylvie's side, one hand firmly clasping hers. Clay was surprised. There was something so childlike about Sylvie he had never considered the possibility that she might have children of her own. Clay followed them but not for long as Sylvie's car was parked nearby. He knew he could not get back to his own car in time to go after her. He had no choice but to watch her drive away.

Clay walked slowly back the way he had come. So many questions crowded into his mind. Was the little girl in fact Sylvie's? Who was the father? Was she married to the father? Clay remembered Uncle Bert's conjecture about Sylvie's being after child support. Was it possible that Bec was the father of the little girl he had seen? She had dark, wavy hair like Bec's, but so did Sylvie. Pete said Bec had been married. Was it to Sylvie? So many questions.

Clay spent the rest of the day wandering around the northwest end of Trident Beach. As he had guessed, most of the year-round residents lived in this area. It was a pleasant place to walk and think away from the insistence of the wind and waves on the beach. Sylvie had never given Clay the details of her relationship with Bec. Had they been lovers? Although Clay wasn't sure he really wanted to know, he felt he had to find out. But how? He certainly couldn't ask Sylvie. He'd have to find some way of getting it out of Bec without arousing suspicion. 'No small feat,' he thought to himself.

An opportunity presented itself sooner than Clay had expected. The next morning when Clay entered the writing room to begin typing he found Bec already seated at one of the long tables.

"You're at it early this morning."

"Yeah, I wanted to go through some of this old stuff," Bec said pawing through the contents of a large cardboard box. "There are some notes in here I thought I might use in the new book. At least I think they're in here."

Clay could see several old photographs surfacing in the debris. Seizing the moment, he looked over Bec's shoulder.

"Were these taken during the sixties?" Clay asked.

"Yeah, sixties—early seventies. Jeez, look at that hair," Bec laughed holding up a picture of himself. Clay noticed it looked very much like the one Sylvie had given him. "Ah, yes," Bec continued in a W.C. Fields voice, "photographs—guardians of time—purveyors of the bittersweet." Bec leafed through the old photos. "You know, somehow I thought things would always be like this—that they wouldn't change again."

"What do you mean?" Clay asked.

"Oh, you know—peace, love, long hair—all that. There was a feeling to those times—a hope, an openness that I thought was here to stay. I guess I forgot about the pendulum on the backswing from the fifties. God, whatever became of sit-ins, be-ins, love-ins, happenings? Oh, for the days when I had nothing more pressing on my mind than where to part my hair," Bec sighed.

"I'm afraid I was too young to really know what was happening then," Clay said.

"Things were different," Bec mused. "The lines were drawn—the lines were drawn..."

"I'm kind of sorry I missed it," Clay said.

"Jeez," Bec shook himself back to the present, "when nostalgia hits, you know the thing being reminisced over is truly gone."

"Old girlfriends?" Clay asked pointing toward several pictures Bec had set aside.

"Huh? Oh, yeah."

"Nice," Clay indicated a photo of a girl with long, blonde hair.

"Yeah, I think her name was Shirley or Sara or something. And that one's Diane—I remember her," Bec pointed to the picture next to the blonde.

"How about that one?" Clay asked nodding toward a photo of a dark-haired girl he recognized as a younger Sylvie.

"Uh, Sylvia—no—Sylvie—that's right Sylvie."

"Sylvie? Kind of an unusual name."

"Yeah, she was kind of different. That was a long time ago. Can you believe that, I can't even remember her last name," Bec shook his head.

"Well, they say the memory's the first thing to go," Clay tried to remain nonchalant.

"Thanks, that's reassuring," Bec laughed.

For the rest of the day, Clay concentrated on his typing—trying to push everything else to the back of his head. That night lying in bed, he let open the floodgates for Sylvie and the events of the past two days to rush into his conscious mind.

At least some of the questions had been answered. Bec said he had known Sylvie a long time ago. The child with her in Philadelphia, only about four, couldn't be his. Bec couldn't remember her last name, could barely remember her first name. There was a guilelessness about Bec that made Clay sure he was telling the truth. If they had been lovers it had obviously not been a deep nor significant relationship—at least not as far as Bec was concerned. Clay wondered if Bec had just had so many women in the intervening years that they obscured his memories of Sylvie. She seemed so deeply impressed by Bec and whatever had taken place between them.

In a way, Clay was relieved at what he had learned but he wondered how Sylvie would feel if she knew. He hoped she would never ask if Bec remembered or spoke of her. What could he say without hurting her? He felt he had to protect her. He knew Sylvie was several years older than he but somehow she seemed younger—so vulnerable. Clay couldn't define what he felt for Sylvie. Perhaps it was what had been missing in his previous relationships with women—chemistry, fate? He had been a sometime believer in destiny—yes, perhaps that's what it was.

Clay let his mind wander over what Bec had said about the past. Clay had always harbored a vague feeling that he'd been born a bit too late. Hearing Bec talk about the sixties he wished he'd been old enough to experience them. He doubly resented his older brothers for being there but rejecting the era. Clay wondered why he couldn't either be like his brothers—rigid and certain—or like Bec and really not give a damn.

The rest of the week passed much as the last three had: typing, reading, walks on the beach, Bec's friends stopping by. Clay grew accustomed to Mr. Suey's nocturnal wanderings up and down the hall. Each week saw fewer people around Trident Beach as the town slowly buried itself deeper in the off-season. Clay realized he was beginning to measure time not as most people did from weekend to weekend, but from Wednesday to Wednesday.

CHAPTER XII

And finally Wednesday came again. As before Clay gave Sylvie a day-by-day account of the past week. He carefully omitted the conversation about the sixties and Sylvie's photograph. He had never been one of those people who consider cruelty and honesty synonymous, who confuse brutality with reality. It was a chilly day and Sylvie was wearing a dark tweed suit and russet silk blouse. On another woman the outfit might have looked sophisticated or businesslike but sitting across the table Clay couldn't shake the impression of a little girl dressing up in her mother's clothes. He wanted to reach out and touch her cheek, brush the hair back from her dark eyes. 'Maybe someday,' he thought.

When Sylvie left the restaurant, Clay paid the check quickly and followed her again at a safe distance. This time Clay had planned ahead and parked his car near Lady Anne's School of Dance. When Sylvie and the little girl emerged from the building Clay was ready. When they drove away he followed just far enough back so she wouldn't see him. After a few blocks Clay realized it was not going to be as easy as he had thought. Trying to weave through city traffic, keep her in sight without being noticed—finally he lost her at a red light. 'Damn,' he thought, 'they make it look so easy on television.'

The next week was a busy one full of comings and goings. It seemed Bec's friends were in and out of the house more than usual. Bec had planned to spend the weekend in New York City but Lydia cancelled again. Bec assuaged his disappointment on Friday night with a tall blonde named Claudia. Clay could hear "Moondance" playing faintly on the stereo below as he fell asleep that night.

Clay spent Saturday typing. He was able to hear most of what was being said in Bec's living room across the hall. Pete and Michael spent the afternoon at Bec's—Pete to get away from his family for a little while, Michael presumably because he had nothing better to do.

"How'd you do at the Westside last night?" Clay heard Pete ask Michael.

"She was okay—nothing an astrological sign transplant couldn't cure."

"What about Claudia?" Pete asked Bec.

"Oh, she's okay I guess. Sometimes she seems like she really knows what's going on. Other times she kind of acts like an idiot," Bec replied.

"Well, maybe she's an oxy-moron," Michael smiled.

"Oh, please," Bec groaned.

"Hey, did you hear what happened to Arnie?" Pete asked.

"Now what?" Bec raised an eyebrow.

"Grace kicked him out last night."

"Again?" Bec and Michael asked in chorus.

"Yeah, she came home early and caught him playing in-the-door-and-out-the-window."

"Cheating on her in their own house? That guy's gall puts stretch marks on my credulity," Bec laughed. "Who was he with?"

"Regina," Pete answered.

"Regina Farrell?"

"Yeah, that's right."

"Ah, the feral Ms. Farrell," Michael interjected.

"Doesn't that guy ever learn?" Bec laughed in disbelief. At that point in the conversation Arnie arrived.

"Well, if it isn't Mr. Non Compos in the Mentis," Michael greeted him. "I hear you were caught with your delicto in flagrante."

"Why can't you just speak English, Kendrick?" Arnie growled.

"Grace is really pissed, huh?" Bec asked.

"No lie," Arnie answered.

"Why'd you two ever get married?" Pete asked. Clay couldn't hear Arnie's reply.

"Marriage of convenience?" Michael suggested.

"Aren't they all?" Clay thought he heard an uncharacteristic cynicism in Bec's voice.

"So have you learned anything from your latest escapade?" Michael needled Arnie.

"Yeah, life's too short for button-fly pants," Arnie replied.

The others laughed and they all continued talking for awhile. Clay, still typing, enjoyed being able to listen to them without being right in the middle of things expected to contribute something to the conversation. He was sorry when someone turned up the music putting an end to his eavesdropping but at least the music was good. Steely Dan, again.

There was a mass exodus around five o'clock and Clay was left to finish his typing in the now quiet house. At six, Clay walked the two blocks to the beach. There was a fine, soft breeze blowing off the water—unexpectedly mild for that time of day and that time of year. Clay was surprised to see Mr. Suey standing atop one of the small dunes looking out to sea.

"Mr. Suey?" Clay said tentatively approaching the old man.

"Ah, Mr. Trinian, I was just thinking this might be a good place for my monument."

"Monument?"

"Yes, I can't decide between marble and granite."

"What kind of a monument?" Clay asked.

"Oh, a monument to me of course."

Clay raised his eyebrows.

Mr. Suey continued, "After all that's what we're all looking for isn't it—immortality. The young cry out to be recognized, the old to be remembered." The expression on his face changed and he came slowly down from atop the dune. "A walk up the beach, Mr. Trinian?"

"Sure," Clay fell in with Mr. Suey's slow, measured step.

"Wonderful time of year, isn't it? Not so many people. Best time of year. Soon they'll be trundling me off to my daughter's house in Florida for the winter."

"You come back here every summer?" Clay asked.

"Every spring, summer, and fall," Mr. Suey answered emphatically. "There's no place I'd rather be than here. It'll get you too before you know it," he winked at Clay.

"Beg pardon?" Clay asked.

Mr. Suey made an abstract gesture toward the ocean with his outstretched arm. "It'll seduce you, creep up on you, get under your skin and before you know it you won't want to be anywhere else—will do almost anything to be able to live near it. Maybe I'll have to buy you a boat, Mr. Trinian. What kind would you like?"

"Oh, I don't know—you can surprise me."

"Perfect! Perfect!"

Clay returned to the house quite late that night. The place was quiet except for the stereo. Eric Carmen was playing. Clay guessed Marianne must be in the house. He found he had been right as her sweet smile greeted him in the kitchen the next morning. Bec seemed somewhat hung over but Marianne was as cheerful as ever. Feeling he might be intruding, Clay grabbed a cup of coffee and headed for the beach.

Clay mused as he walked along the sand—Marianne, the tall blonde, Claudia, Lydia in New York, and who could know how many others. Most of all, Sylvie's interest in him after so many years. 'Why are women so attracted to men like Bec?' Clay asked himself. No, that wasn't the real question. The real question was why wasn't he more like Bec?

Bec and his friends were in and out during the rest of that Sunday. Clay began to wish for the peace that filled the house during the weekdays. That night he was somewhat troubled to learn that Arnie would be staying in the room next to his, at least until Grace cooled off. From what Pete said, Clay gathered this was hardly the first time Arnie had stayed at Bec's. Clay felt uneasy having Arnie in such close proximity. He seemed to view Clay with a suspicious eye. Perhaps it was just his imagination Clay thought or guilty conscience at spying on Bec for Sylvie. Or perhaps it was as Bec had said—Arnie just enjoyed giving everybody a hard time.

Clay was relieved when Monday morning came. Arnie left for work and the routine of writing and typing resumed. Clay found himself looking forward to Wednesday. It was becoming increasingly difficult for him to remember what it had been like before Sylvie. It seemed she had always been in his life—or at least in his thoughts.

CHAPTER XIII

Wednesday was a brilliant, autumn day. Most of September and October had brought exceptionally good weather. There had been a couple hurricane scares but the storms had veered in time to give the Jersey shore only a few rainy, windy days. Everyone up and down the beach said it was a lucky year. 'A lucky year,' Clay thought as he drove on toward Philadelphia.

This time Clay decided he was going to take a more aggressive, direct approach with Sylvie. He had a plan. He would follow Sylvie out of the restaurant again and wait until she had picked up the little girl at her dancing school. Then he would bump into them—sheer coincidence of course—and invite them to have ice cream. He thought the child would like that. Then while she enjoyed her treat he would engage Sylvie in some sort of meaningful, personal conversation. Clay had it all worked out in his mind, if only he could be brave enough to go through with it. Perhaps the need he felt to get closer to Sylvie would give him the courage.

Clay entered Mallary's at exactly two o'clock and was shown to his regular table at the back. By this time he knew the menu better than the waitress did, but he delayed ordering hoping Sylvie would show up in a few minutes. After ten minutes Clay ordered a cup of coffee. After another ten minutes, a salad—then a bowl of soup. Where was she? Finally he ordered the main course. By the time it came, it was nearly three o'clock. She had been late before but she had always shown up. What had happened? Clay began to imagine all sorts of scenarios ranging from a traffic accident to a decision not to pursue the Billy Becton case any further. He feigned interest in the food before him as it gave him a reason for remaining at the table. He couldn't leave the restaurant when she might still come. He had no other way of getting in touch with her. A chunk of steak stuck in his throat as he thought of never seeing her again. Wait—maybe there was a way—'Lady Anne's'—maybe she was there right now with the little girl. Just as Clay was about to put this newest thought into action, Sylvie entered the restaurant.

Bypassing the hostess, she rushed straight to Clay's table. Before Clay could even get halfway out of his chair, Sylvie had hurriedly seated herself across the table from him. She was very agitated, even more nervous than the first time they met in Uncle Bert's office. Clay could sense this even before she spoke in a breathy whisper.

"I'm so sorry I'm late—I'm so sorry," she seemed quite frantic, the look in her eyes that of an animal about to be trapped.

"It's all right." Clay reached across the table and patted her hand hoping to calm her. Unfortunately the gesture had just the opposite effect. Sylvie seemed on the point of bolting from her seat. Her eyes darted about the room as if she were afraid of being discovered at something.

"I'm sorry, I didn't mean to upset you," Clay apologized withdrawing his hand quickly.

"No, it's all right—it's just that I don't have much time—I really can't stay," she managed all in one breath. "I just didn't want you to think I wasn't going to come at all—but I really don't have time to hear your report this week—I'm so sorry you had to come here for nothing—but I really can't stay—please forgive me," Sylvie checked her watch, jumped up from the table, "I'm sorry—I'm so sorry."

Clay was speechless. He had never seen her like this. But he recovered quickly, paid the check, and dashed out of Mallary's into the street. She was gone. Clay hurried, hoping to catch her at the dancing school. Perhaps he could even salvage his original plan when she emerged with the girl. He waited at the corner for a moment or two. Sylvie appeared, then the little girl holding her hand. Clay started forward but stopped in mid-step. Holding the child's other hand was a man in a dark raincoat. Clay felt paralyzed. Nothing worked but his eyes—and they worked all too well, etching the brief scene into his brain.

The little girl seemed perfectly at ease walking hand-in-hand between them, babbling happily to one then the other. They walked the short distance to the car Clay had seen Sylvie in a week earlier. But this time the man was driving as the car pulled out and merged into the flow of traffic. The man—Clay had no doubt he must be the child's father. Average height, solid, compact, dark curly hair, olive skin. An air of the foreign about him, a seriousness in his bearing that made him appear older than Clay guessed he probably was. All this hit Clay in the few moments he stood transfixed at the corner. All this and something else—that the man must be Sylvie's husband.

Clay wandered around the same three or four blocks surrounding Mallary's but all he could see was the man, woman, and child walking to their car. When Clay got back to his own car it was close to five o'clock. For once Clay was thankful to be caught in the rush hour. He gave over his full attention to navigating through the heavy traffic. There would be plenty of time to think once he got back to Trident Beach.

Clay had to admit that he didn't really know Sylvie—just the glimpses she had allowed him at their weekly meetings. Mostly it was the image of her he had fabricated for himself in his imagination. She had never said she wasn't married, he had just wanted desperately to believe that she wasn't. As he fell onto his bed that night, Clay felt dog-tired, drained, but mostly, unreasonably, betrayed.

CHAPTER XIV

The light of day crept across the sky, across the room, across the bed. Clay watched as the dawn's gray edged out the black. He got up, dressed quietly, and slipped down the stairs and out the front door. He wasn't ready to talk to Bec yet—and hoped to avoid Arnie altogether. Clay thought the wind and the sound of the waves might push Sylvie from his mind. When he returned from a long walk on the beach, Bec was already going through notebooks in the writing room.

"I was beginning to wonder what had happened to you," Bec smiled.

"Just felt like I needed a walk this morning—sorry I'm late," Clay said half-heartedly.

"No problem. Trouble with your Wednesday rendezvous?" Bec asked picking up on Clay's mood.

"Hmm—I don't know, I just don't know..." Clay trailed off.

"What—did she turn up with a migraine or something?" Bec joked.

"No, nothing like that—I mean it's not that kind of relationship," Clay stammered.

"Ah, an 'affair de coeur'?"

Clay shrugged noncommittally.

"You have to watch out for 'la grande passion'," Bec continued, "it'll eat you alive."

"So what's your solution?"

"Me? Easy—I just love 'em all," Bec laughed.

"Oh, and does that stem from a need to feel in control rather than vice versa?" Clay asked mimicking a thick German accent.

"Enough with the Psych. 101, okay?" Bec laughed, again. "You'll understand in a few years—when you're not so Jung."

"Oh, no," Clay groaned.

"Sorry, that was pretty bad. Anyway, it'll all work out—you'll see."

"What'll all work out?" Clay asked.

"Everything—life, ladies—the whole thing," Bec smiled extending his arms to encompass the universe of Clay's future. Bec paused for a moment assessing Clay from across the room. "I think what you really need is a good dose of Vitamin F."

"Vitamin F?" Clay looked puzzled.

Bec nodded with a knowing smile.

"Ohhh, maybe you're right," Clay smiled back.

The rest of the day went as usual, writing and typing. Clay found that at least Bec's company brought his mood up to a tolerable level of depression. He was sorry when the work day ended and he was left to his own thoughts.

Thursday evening seemed endless. Clay tried to escape into a murder mystery. Friday night he went out to dinner and a movie. 'Married—why does she have to be married?' Maybe it wasn't a happy marriage. It didn't matter, she was still married, Clay argued with himself.

She had rushed out of Mallary's without saying anything about another meeting the following Wednesday. Perhaps he might never see her again. Perhaps that would be best.

By Saturday morning Clay had decided to do what he usually did with problems having no immediate resolution. He shoved them to the back burner of his mind to let them simmer awhile and see what developed. Most of the day was spent alone in the writing room, editing and typing. A little past five Bec and Michael showed up followed soon after by Pete then Arnie with the Regina Farrell Clay had heard about. Everyone was in a great mood. Even Arnie seemed a shade lighter than usual.

"We're gonna have a party!" Bec clapped his hands together. "Clay, you're in on this, too," he yelled from the hallway.

"I'm not sure I'm up to that," Clay said remembering the crowd scene at Bec's last party.

"Don't worry, it's just going to be a few people—a small gathering this time—you'll see." As usual Bec seemed to be reading his mind.

"Now, let's get organized," Bec raised his arms as if orchestrating the plan. "Pete, you're going to pick up Polly?" Pete nodded moving toward the front door.

"Michael, you're picking up..."

"Randy," Michael supplied the name following Pete out the door.

"Arnie, do you and Regina want to go on a beer run?"

"Definitely. Come on, Regina."

"Well, Clay, that leaves you and me to go on pizza patrol."

Clay and Bec were the last ones to return. Arnie was stretched out in one of the old armchairs in the living room. Regina perched on one of the chair's arms. Arnie seemed to have gotten a head-start on the beer. Pete and Polly sat on the sofa across the room. This was the first time Clay had seen Pete's wife. She wasn't at all what he had expected. Clay couldn't imagine a couple appearing more mismatched. Pete was of medium height, on the skinny side, determinedly average in just about every respect. In contrast, Polly was poised and extremely well-groomed, coifed, and dressed. She was not really what Clay would have called beautiful, but she had obviously taken great pains to make herself look as good as she possibly could. Mostly, she reminded Clay of the lesser luminaries in the beauty contests his sister had entered. Throughout the evening Clay noticed that Polly's smile never slipped although she seemed fairly uncomfortable and thoroughly out of place.

Randy turned out to be a stunning redhead. She and Michael were in a huddle over the stereo. Clay and Bec walked through to the kitchen to deposit the pizzas. Marianne was sitting at the kitchen table. As usual Clay couldn't help but return her sweet smile. There was another girl seated at the table with Marianne. Bec introduced her to Clay as Judy Camasara. There seemed to be something in Bec's introduction that suggested he was presenting this Judy as a gift to Clay. As the evening progressed Clay realized he had not been mistaken in this impression. Apparently Judy was Bec's attempt at bringing Clay out of the doldrums. It seemed that almost everyone else was in on the plan. Pete, Michael, and

Marianne kept sneaking conspiratorial glances at Clay and his 'date'. At one point, Arnie leaned over and whispered, "So how ya doin' with Judy Kamasutra?"

For her part Judy seemed a willing participant in the play. However, Clay couldn't escape the feeling that she was here more as a favor to Bec than for any other reason. Normally, Clay would have felt trapped in such a situation. He didn't usually appreciate being fixed up sight unseen. But Judy was easy enough to talk to—an adequate but undemanding conversationalist—just what Clay was up to that evening. Physically she was tall, thin, pale—a little weary around the eyes, a little hard around the mouth but passably pleasant. Clay was relieved as he definitely didn't feel up to trying to impress a raving beauty this evening.

The night wore on. Arnie got quietly drunk surprisingly—the quiet not the drunk. Regina seemed not to notice until around eleven when she helped him up the stairs to the room next to Clay's. Polly seized the opportunity to head for the front door with Pete in tow. Bec and Marianne were in the kitchen, Michael and Randy at the far end of the living room arguing about twentieth century art when Judy Camasara suggested Clay show her his room.

Clay had drunken just enough to put him on the edge of recklessness. He felt like blowing away the events of the past week. Clay could see why Arnie had called her Judy Kamasutra. It was clear what she had in mind. He didn't resist. The hell with Sylvie, her husband, and everything connected with her. The mattress springs applauded wildly as they tumbled onto the bed. Judy undressed him playfully but efficiently. The alcohol began to throb in his head competing with the throbbing as he entered her. The light from the bedside table glinted off her necklace. It caught at the sweaty places on her neck and chest like a wriggling, silver snake. The hell with Sylvie. The hell with Arnie and Regina one paper-thin wall away. The hell with everything and everyone thought Clay as he exploded into Judy and into the night.

Clay awoke the next morning to bright sunlight streaming through the front windows. Shielding his tender eyes from the glare he checked his watch. It was eight-ten. He was alone. He vaguely remembered Judy saying something about having to leave early for work at a diner inland. By the cars on the street, Clay could tell that Bec, Marianne, Arnie, and probably Regina were in the house but most likely still asleep. He crept down the stairs through the quiet and out into the sunshine. Clay spent some time with the sea before going on to breakfast. He was relieved he had been able to slip out of the house unnoticed without comment about last night. He didn't regret Judy but he didn't want to talk about it. He knew that he would probably never see her again and that that would be fine with both of them.

Clay stayed out most of the day. When he did return after dinner the house was empty. It wasn't until the next morning in the writing room that he saw Bec again. To Clay's relief he found Bec was not into kiss and tell. Bec's only comment on Clay's encounter with Judy was a sly smile. Michael and Pete never made mention of it. Although Arnie never actually said anything about

Judy, Clay sensed a slight change in his attitude after that night. While he knew he and Arnie would never be close friends, Clay was grateful that he at least seemed less openly hostile after that point.

Bec spent a good part of the morning talking about Randy, the redhead Michael had shown up with on Saturday night, and about Michael's luck with women in general.

"She's a new face, none of us had ever seen her before. I don't know where he finds them."

"So Michael has quite a way with the ladies?" Clay asked in spite of himself.

"That's a definite understatement," Bec laughed, "I've never seen anything like it. That guy's had more women than a character in one of my stories."

"Maybe you should write a book about him," Clay offered.

"Right! He'd probably kill me. Besides, Michael's never liked talking about that sort of thing..." Bec trailed off, his mind wandering.

Clay went back to typing, trying to reconcile this image of Michael the womanizer with the Michael Kendrick he had met. Michael still seemed a shadowy figure, he gave much less away about himself than Bec's other friends. Pete had from the first been a completely open book. Even with his lack of congeniality, Arnie was easier to get a handle on. Except for what Bec had told him about Michael, Clay had nothing to go on but the physical facade. The expensive clothes and car. Fairly tall, slim, dark brown slightly curly hair, regular features and dark eyes set off by tortoise shell-framed glasses. He certainly wasn't bad looking but Clay couldn't imagine just what it was that attracted such astounding numbers of women to him. But then he wasn't a woman—perhaps it was something only they would know.

During the rest of that day and the next Clay tried to concentrate on his typing and editing, but in the back of his mind the question of Sylvie was working. He didn't know if she would show up at Mallary's again. He wasn't sure he really wanted to see her. He didn't think so. But by the time Wednesday came Clay had decided he needed to make the trip into Philadelphia one more time. He had to satisfy himself that either she wasn't coming again or if she did, to call it quits himself.

CHAPTER XV

In the past Clay had been early for their meetings prodded by enthusiasm at the thought of seeing Sylvie. Today he arrived at Mallary's entrance at ten after two. He thought about not going in at all but pushed himself through the swinging doors wanting to make an end of it. The hostess smiled and showed him to his table.

Clay was shocked to find Sylvie already seated, waiting for him. He stood dumbfounded for a few seconds before managing to seat himself. Somehow he had not expected this. He had also not expected the way he would feel at seeing her again, at hearing her voice. She seemed as vibrant as the autumn day outside. She apologized profusely for their abbreviated meeting of the week before pleading a schedule conflict. Of course Clay could not let on that he knew what that conflict was. She said she had been afraid that he might not show up after last Wednesday. Her eyes begged like a child's for forgiveness. Clay couldn't deny her. He was almost flattered until he remembered the real reason she wanted to stay in contact with him. As always she was eager for news of Bec. He fed her selected tidbits from the past two weeks, watching her eyes shine at the mention of Becton's name.

At three-twenty Sylvie rose to leave. Impulsively she took Clay's hand and shook it gratefully.

"I was so afraid you wouldn't come today. Thank you so much. Will I see you next Wednesday?" she asked hopefully.

Clay nodded his head dumbly as he watched her walk from the table. Almost from habit, he paid the check quickly and followed her unseen as he had done before. There was no husband today, just the little girl. The pink leotard and tights had been replaced by black and little cat ears perched on her head. Clay had forgotten about Halloween.

On the drive back to Trident Beach Clay had to remind himself to pay attention to the traffic. How could this have happened? When he started out that morning he had been ready to end it. Now driving back he realized he would see her again and again. He knew he must be crazy. She was married. She was interested in Bec, not him. It didn't matter. He knew now he had only been fooling himself thinking he had some control over what he felt for Sylvie. It was some hunger that could only be satisfied by her presence, some deep need that he did not even know existed within him until he met her.

Clay's pensive mood went unnoticed the next day as Bec was preoccupied planning for a weekend in New York City with Lydia. Bec took off early on Friday leaving Clay alone with the typewriter and his thoughts. Clay filled Saturday evening playing cards with Mr. Suey. He found it quite a challenge. While Mr. Suey was scrupulously honest about following the rules, he tended to forget what they were playing halfway through and start in on a different game.

Clay had Sunday to himself. He spent most of it walking around the north end of town which he learned was called 'The Greens' presumably for the well-manicured, postage stamp-sized lawns and carefully coaxed landscaping. Clay felt oddly at home and yet uncomfortable all at the same time in this sheltered neighborhood. He let his mind wander as he walked. How could it be November already? He'd been living in Bec's house, working with him for six weeks now. It all seemed so natural—the job, the room, being so close to the ocean. If only he could resolve something with regard to Sylvie.

Looking out to sea a thought flashed through Clay's mind. Revenge. What if the real reason Sylvie wanted to find Bec was revenge? He imagined her with gun in hand confronting Bec. No, the whole thing was too ridiculous. But still the idea haunted him through the rest of the afternoon, made him uneasy. Was he just a tool in a vendetta? Clay squirmed at the thought of being a part of such a scenario. No, he told himself—Sylvie seemed too genuinely thrilled at any news of Becton. There had to be another reason for Sylvie's fascination with him.

***

Bec was positively bubbling when he entered the writing room late Monday morning.

"I take it you had a great weekend," Clay greeted him.

"Great! Great! Tango—tango all night long!" Bec danced around the room with an invisible partner.

"Lydia must really be something special."

"Yeah, she is. Who knows, maybe someday... well, who knows. Now let's get to work," Bec clapped his hands together.

The next two weeks passed fairly uneventfully. Clay enjoyed the routine of his job, walks on the beach, stops at Braeden's and Mauro's bakery. He found himself living more and more from Wednesday to Wednesday.

The week before Thanksgiving Sylvie told Clay she would not be able to meet him for lunch the next week. She offered no explanation but Clay figured it probably meant there was no dancing class the day before the holiday. He was grateful that she had bridged the gap into December by proposing they meet the following week. He was thankful for any time he could spend with her. He wished there were some way he could be a more important part of her life but he knew he had to be content with Wednesdays at least for now. Each meeting reinforced his feelings for her. He had to have a piece of her life, no matter how small.

CHAPTER XVI

The weekend before Thanksgiving was a busy one in Bec's circle. On Friday Lydia arrived from New York. On Friday night everyone piled into Michael's and Clay's cars and headed for Atlantic City. Clay followed the others into a couple of the casinos. After playing a few slot machines and meandering through the black jack maze he spent most of the evening wandering up and down the boardwalk admiring its length and construction. He remembered the stories Bec had told of the old Atlantic City and he tried to imagine what it must have been like but it was difficult with no frame of reference. Finally the cool breeze across the wide beach drove him into the casino where he had last seen Bec and Lydia.

On Saturday night, an impromptu birthday party was planned for Arnie who had turned thirty-five the week before. As usual, the guest of honor was drunk halfway through the evening. Bec devoted most of his time to Lydia. Clay found her pretty and pleasant enough but missed Marianne who had obviously bowed out because of Lydia's presence. Clay wondered how much Lydia knew about Bec's female following in Trident Beach.

Clay awoke in the middle of the night to the sound of muffled sobs coming through the thin wall that separated his room from Arnie's. At first he thought it was Regina, but in the quiet of the house he could soon tell that it was Arnie. He couldn't quite make out the choked syllables that punctuated the sobbing nor Regina's soothing words that followed. In the morning Clay couldn't be entirely sure that it had not all been a dream.

Clay tried to stay out of the house most of Sunday to give Bec and Lydia time to themselves. When he returned in the evening he found the living room and kitchen free of any sign of Saturday's festivities. Michael no doubt, he thought. As he walked through the hallway to the back of the house, Clay was surprised to hear Eric Carmen on the stereo. The reason greeted him in the kitchen—Marianne's sweet smile. Somehow the atmosphere in Bec's house seemed completed by her presence, however, Clay was surprised to find her here so soon after Lydia's departure.

"Bec asked me to bring these books over for him," she smiled, reading Clay's expression.

"Hey, where've you been all day?' Bec wandered in from the bedroom across the hallway.

"Out on the beach mostly," Clay answered.

"You missed the big news. Arnie's gone back to his wife and kids."

"Will wonders never cease?" Marianne added sarcastically.

On Monday Mr. Suey's daughter and granddaughter came to pack up his things for the trip to Florida for the winter. At one point during the day Clay and Bec looked in to see if they could be of help. The two women seemed to have things well in hand. Mr. Suey sitting forlornly on the edge of the bed simply shook his head. Later Clay shook hands with the old man on the front porch as he prepared to leave.

"Well, at least you'll still be close to the ocean," Clay tried to console him.

"Yes, but it's just not the same down there," he smiled sadly.

Clay had become accustomed to Mr. Suey's presence in the house, his nocturnal wanderings, his chiaroscuro mental state. He knew he would miss the old gentleman and silently wished him well as the daughter's big Buick pulled away from the curb.

***

Clay tried to pretend that Wednesday was just another day. He decided to work as he didn't have any good reason for being off. The thought of a Wednesday without seeing Sylvie made him uneasy. At least she had agreed to meet him the following week. Another whole week away.

"Have you got anything planned for Thanksgiving tomorrow?" Bec asked Clay as they sat at the kitchen table eating lunch.

"No, I really hadn't thought much about it," Clay answered. He had been too busy thinking about Sylvie, or rather about not seeing her that week.

"My mother called the other day and we're having the annual gathering at my aunt's house near Grant's Landing. You're welcome to come."

"I wouldn't want to intrude on your family."

"You won't be—besides it'll give me someone to talk to."

"Okay, I'll try to make a good impression," Clay smiled.

"Believe me, you couldn't do any worse than Arnie. I took him with me last year because he and Grace were having problems. He took one of my aunt's fancy napkin rings home with him—thought it was a party favor."

Clay couldn't be sure if Bec was joking or not, but they both laughed. "Sure, why not—thanks," Clay agreed to the invitation.

Clay and Bec arrived at Bec's aunt's house around noon. The large, Victorian-style house sat by itself in a small clearing, a narrow creek running behind it. Usually a fan of that type of architecture, Clay found the aspect of this particular house repellent. There was something uninviting, almost eerie about the place. Although the leaves had fallen from the hardwoods, the scrubby pines conspired to give the surrounding woods a dark, forbidding air. As they climbed the front steps Clay thought that this might have been a better place to celebrate Halloween than Thanksgiving.

The interior of the house was well supplied with handsome antiques but the decorator had shown a dark, heavy hand with regard to color and texture. The rusty smell of chrysanthemums was everywhere. Despite the house's overall size, its low-ceilinged rooms seemed to close in on one. The group of nine seemed like much more milling around in the confining living and dining rooms.

Clay liked Bec's mother, Harriet, immediately. A trifle scatter-brained, she was warm, funny and tolerant. Clay found he didn't have to worry about feeling uncomfortable with the rest of Bec's family. They seemed to be uncomfortable enough with each other. Besides Bec's mother and the aunt hosting the dinner there were another aunt, recently widowed, an uncle and his wife and two unmarried sons. The hostess, Bec's aunt Gweny, was not at all what Clay had expected. She was much younger than Bec's mother, perhaps mid-forties. She was tall, slim, with full wavy auburn hair surrounding a narrow, white face. She was very attractive, even seductive, but Clay found her a bit too sophisticated for his taste. After dessert she latched onto him her dark, flashing eyes holding him fast. Visions of the ancient mariner flooded Clay's mind. There was something in those eyes, something not quite right –a bit off-balance—that sent a feeling through him. He realized it was fear and was relieved when Bec said it was time to go.

"Sorry about Aunt Gweny," Bec apologized as they pulled out of the driveway. "She gets a little intense sometimes. Someone new to talk to I guess."

"No problem," Clay assured him but secretly hoped he wouldn't run into Aunt Gweny again.

Throughout the day Clay's mind had wandered to Sylvie. He wondered if she were part of a large family celebration or alone with her husband and daughter. He could only guess as he knew nothing of her home nor family. He hoped that she was happy on this holiday.

Bec spent the rest of the long weekend in New York City with Lydia. With Mr. Suey in Florida and Arnie back to family life Clay had the house to himself. When he had first arrived at Bec's Clay felt uncomfortable being alone in the big, old house. He found his feelings had changed. Now it seemed he belonged there, that the house had accepted him.

Clay lingered over breakfast and the Sunday paper. From where he sat at the kitchen table he could see the door to Bec's bedroom across the hallway, carelessly left half-open. Clay thought back to the first time he had been left alone in the house and how he had been tempted to enter that room and search through Bec's belongings. He hadn't then for fear of being discovered at it. He knew he couldn't now because he had come to know and like Bec and felt that it would be betraying a trust.

Clay spent the weekend practicing his culinary skills, watching old movies, and taking long walks on the beach. He enjoyed being out and near the ocean despite the cool, breezy weather. At first Clay had found it strange that Bec and his friends were so attracted to the shore but didn't seem interested in any water sports—boating, surfing, windsurfing. Now he understood that it didn't matter. It was just a feeling, being near the ocean, like a magnetic force and he could feel it pulling at him, too.

CHAPTER XVII

As usual, Bec was jubilant after the weekend with Lydia. He launched into his writing with renewed zest. Clay found it easy to be influenced by Bec's good spirits. After all he would be seeing Sylvie again soon.

Tuesday was dismal—drizzly, raw, and gray. Wednesday did a complete turnaround as if the weather or whatever controlled it knew that this was Clay's day to meet Sylvie. He awoke, or rather the wind awakened him. It was a gusty, purposeful breeze blowing clean—blowing the clutter from the sidewalks, from the mind. Bright sun, brilliant sky. Cool but still warmer than usual for early December.

Lying in bed Clay could feel the wind blowing, stringing a knot of excitement in his stomach. It was the kind of day that made him glad to be alive and awake and to know that the ocean was so near. He felt a push to jump up, run out and fling himself into the wind, into this incredible day. Clay couldn't have endured turning inland, driving away from the water on a day like this had it not been for the fact that he was driving toward Sylvie.

Any doubts he might have had since their last meeting were gone. He had not seen her for two weeks. As he drove toward Philadelphia his mind seemed as clear as this beautiful day. Perhaps today he could find a way to let Sylvie know how he felt about her—a way to divert some of her attention from Bec to himself. He felt invigorated and much more confident than usual.

Sylvie arrived at Mallary's just a few seconds after Clay so they were shown to their table together. Clay was sure it was a good omen for their meeting. Sylvie seemed to have been as affected by the two week absence as Clay had. She was bubbling over. It took a while for her to calm down enough to eat her lunch.

"I really missed our meeting last week," she beamed. "You're the only one I can talk to—I mean you're the only one who knows about Billy. I guess I didn't realize how much I've come to look forward to our meetings. It seemed so strange last Wednesday not being able to talk to you."

Clay smiled and let her babble on, waiting for the perfect moment to present his overture. The two week hiatus had indeed made her eager to talk, even to confide.

"I guess you probably wondered why I always paid you in cash," she ran on. "Well, actually it's because I'm married," she paused waiting for Clay's reaction. He managed to feign mild surprise at her revelation. "I didn't write a check because I really didn't want my husband to know about all this. I mean not that there's anything wrong with it—I just didn't want to have to explain—he wouldn't understand," she continued in the same confidential tone. "When I inherited some money last summer I decided I'd finally find out what had happened to Billy Becton. I'd always wondered what had become of him. You see," she took a quick, shallow breath then plunged on in a secretive whisper, "it is possible to be in love with two people at the same time." She said it definitively as if she had solved some ancient riddle.

For one split-split-second Clay imagined she was talking about Bec and himself. Before his heart made it halfway to his mouth he realized that of course she meant Bec and her husband. Still dazed, he listened as she prattled on.

"I suppose I really shouldn't be telling you all this—but it's so good to be able to talk to someone about it and I know you'll keep it confidential." The floodgates were open, she went on and on, the words tumbling out. "I want you to understand that I really do care for my husband and I would never do anything to hurt him, but then there's Billy. He's always meant something special to me, even all those years when I didn't know where he was."

Clay's hope had turned to numbness and now to anger. He wanted to shake Sylvie and tell her that Bec only vaguely remembered her, that Bec probably did not even believe in the kind of feeling that she had held onto all these years. He wanted to shatter this dream of hers, to make a place for himself in her life. But he couldn't do that. He couldn't hurt her that way. It would be too selfish, too cruel—and he loved her too much for that.

It was still the same perfect, sunny day as Clay drove back to the shore but he didn't notice. His unvented anger and frustration had worn him out and now he only felt limp, used. He had gone to their meeting with high hopes of declaring his feelings for Sylvie. Instead she had turned him into her confidant, declaring her feelings for Bec. She had giggled and blushed and revealed her secrets to Clay as she might have to a trusted girlfriend. That was how she thought of him.

Clay made a point of avoiding Bec for the rest of the day. Jealousy was enough to handle. Coupled with the irony of Bec's obliviousness it was more than Clay could bear. He spent the remainder of the afternoon and part of the evening with the ocean. The next day Clay wanted to be angry with Bec but he found he couldn't be. Bec's good humor won out. Besides, it wasn't Bec's fault—he didn't even know.

***

For the next two weeks Clay went through the motions of the new life he had set up for himself—typing, walks on the beach, an occasional conversation with some of Bec's friends, and of course Wednesdays. He listened to Sylvie go on about the details of her daily life. Now it seemed she felt free to talk to him about anything. Clay enjoyed hearing about what she did during the rest of the week when he did not see her, but didn't care much for the parts that included her husband. He listened to her go on and on about Bec when all he really wanted to do was reach across the table, kiss her pale neck and bury his face in that dark, hyacinth-scented hair. And so he listened and waited. He didn't know what else to do.

On the Wednesday before Christmas, driving back from Philadelphia, Clay felt like he was standing on the edge of the world. Before him stretched a void of three weeks until he would see Sylvie again. The holidays—he laughed bitterly to himself—Christmas, New Year's—days when most people looked forward to spending more time with the people they cared about. But for Clay all it meant was two Wednesdays without Sylvie. Clay tried to be happy for Bec when he announced his plans for the holidays.

"Two weeks—two whole weeks in the Bahamas with Lydia. Big bucks—but it'll be worth it. So what have you got planned for Christmas?"

"I don't know, I guess I'll go home. Home," Clay half-smiled, "I mean to my parents' house. They'll be expecting me—at least my mother will be. I'm not sure anyone else would really notice if I showed up or not."

"Sounds like fun," Bec smiled sarcastically. "You ought to just go somewhere and get away from it all."

"Yeah, maybe next year," Clay sighed.

CHAPTER XVIII

When he closed his eyes, all Clay could see were the dotted white lines of the interstate lanes. He had started out from Trident Beach very early that morning in order to beat the noon-hour traffic around Washington, D.C. He had been lucky. The weather was unusually good for December but still the word that always came to mind for the drive down I-95 and then I-85 into North Carolina was 'grueling'. It was late afternoon when he picked up 15-501 to Chapel Hill. His head and shoulders ached and he was fighting that feeling of floating unreality that sets in after a long drive. Still he wasn't quite ready to face his family. He drove around town for a while trying to collect himself. The crowds of Christmas shoppers forced him to drive slowly but that was okay. There were so many new malls and shopping centers that the area now looked like anywhere else—this place he had thought was so special even if it had seemed to reject him most of his life. Finally, just as it was beginning to get dark, Clay pulled into the driveway of his parents' home. He could have recited the first words out of his mother's mouth, but he just smiled and returned the warm hug she gave him.

"Clay, you look sa' thin, and you're still wearing that same old jacket—doesn't he look thin, Franklin?" she turned for automatic agreement from Clay's father who had just wandered into the front hallway on his way from the living room to the kitchen.

"He looks fine, Cora. How ya been doin', Clay?" he shook his son's hand as he would an acquaintance who had just stopped by rather than a child he had not seen for some time. A good-humored, good-natured man on whom too many years of trying to please others were taking their toll. He seemed to become more of a nonentity each time Clay saw him until Clay had difficulty remembering if there ever had been a time when his father had had a definite personality.

Clay's mother led him into the living room and after getting him situated with drink and snacks went back to her kitchen. Clay knew it would be useless to offer help or even try to talk to her while she was in the midst of her marathon holiday baking plus fixing that evening's supper. She always pushed herself too hard—but especially so at this time of year. She wanted everything to be perfect—clothing, house, decorations, food and her children. However, she had the good sense to realize early on that Clay was never going to fit the form she had used to mold his older brothers. During most of his childhood and adolescence she had exercised a form of benign neglect over Clay for which he was eternally grateful.

"So, how's things in Yankee land?" A loud voice sounded behind Clay. He turned to face his 'twin' brothers. They usually stopped here on their way home from work for a beer and to unwind a little before going home to their wives and children. The older, Matt, was a very successful car salesman while the younger, Benton, sold real estate. They both had the salesman's hustle and ambition that Clay lacked. They were settled, assets to their community—everything that Clay was not. Like their mother, when they finally accepted that Clay was not one of them, they pretty much left him alone. They were polite, civil—that was about it. Matt didn't even bother trying to get Clay to trade in the old Fairlane anymore. After talking business and football with their father for a little while they left for their respective families.

Clay was relieved that supper was a fairly quiet affair that evening. Just Clay, his parents, his younger sister, Lisa, and her boyfriend, Russell. It was hard for Clay to believe that his little sister was a freshman in college. She had grown into a very pretty, young woman—perhaps a little too pretty for her own good. But Clay figured that might be countered by the snotty attitude she seemed to be developing. Russell was about what Clay would have expected—nice enough collegiate type. Clay's mother seemed to harbor some fears that Lisa might be getting too 'serious' about Russell.

"Yeah, mama'n'daddy are afraid I might quit school, run off and get married." From the way Russell looked at Lisa, Clay suspected that might not be his parents' biggest worry.

Clay spent the next day, Christmas Eve Day, doing his Christmas shopping. Nothing like leaving it to the last minute. It gave him a good excuse to be out of the house most of the day. He knew that evening would be a big one at his parents' home.

Christmas Eve. Everyone was there—Matt and Benton with wives and seven children between them. At times, the din was almost deafening. Children running from room to room, screaming, dragging Christmas presents in their wake. Adults shouting across the room to be heard—the television blaring although no one seemed to be watching it. Only Lisa seemed pouty and bored with Russell absent. Clay tried to talk to her but found they had little common ground left. He decided not to push it for fear he might discover he really didn't like her much anymore. The house that had seemed so big when he was growing up now was almost too small for the hoard of grandchildren. Clay wasn't sure he would ever get used to being called 'uncle'.

Finally the house was quiet as all the children were packed off to their own beds to await Santa's arrival. Clay's parents, done in by the noise and activity, retired. At eleven, Clay left Lisa downstairs on the phone with Russell and went to bed himself. Sleeping in his old room, his old bed was some comfort but it also brought back old memories of the frustrations of adolescence, of not fitting in anywhere.

Christmas Day began fairly quietly but picked up speed with the family dinner that afternoon. It was something of a replay of the chaos of the night before only with everyone seated, at least for the most part. It was Christmas, but for Clay it was Wednesday, a Wednesday without Sylvie. He felt isolated and alone in the midst of this group. They all seemed to belong here together. Clay half-wished he could be a member of their circle but knew that he would never be happy in that life. It was the struggle that had gone on inside him ever since he realized he was somehow different from the rest of his family.

Most of the rest of the day was something of a blur. It was ironic Clay thought, that his mother was concerned about his being up North carousing when he had consumed more alcohol in the short time he had been home than he had in several weeks in Trident Beach. He found a slight state of numbness somewhat effective in dealing with his family and his absence from Sylvie. Clay decided that while absence may make the heart grow fonder, it can also make the mind turn in upon itself. The more he tried not to think about Sylvie, the more she seemed to occupy his brain. During the next few days Clay spent as much time as possible out of the house, mostly just driving around town or wandering about the university campus. He thought about calling one of the few close friends he used to have in the area to see if they were still around or home for the holidays, too. But he decided it was one of those things better left undone.

Finally when he could endure it no longer, feigning plans for New Year's Eve, Clay made good his escape back to Trident Beach. Bec and Lydia would not be back for another week so he would have the house to himself—or almost. As it turned out, Pete and Arnie made fairly regular stops at Bec's house. Pete didn't seem to mind at all that Clay was there. Even Arnie seemed to be coming around a bit. Bec's place was a haven, a safe harbor where they could escape from wives, children and the rest of the world, at least for a little while. Clay found he really didn't mind the intrusions on his solitude. These old friends of Bec's had almost become like old friends of his own. Only Michael was missing. Pete said he had gone to spend the holidays with his mother in Paris. Just as well, Clay thought. At least their visits forced him not to think about Sylvie all the time.

New Year's Day. Another damn Wednesday. It would be another whole week before he could see her again. Clay had declined an invitation from Pete to a party the night before. He hadn't felt much like celebrating. Instead he saw the old year out by taking a walk on the beach, reading, getting half-drunk and going to bed early. He decided he wanted to be unconscious when the new year crept in. Now on the first day of a new year he found himself standing on the sand looking out at the ocean. Clay was glad to be back in Trident Beach. He was beginning to feel at home in this town, in Bec's house, with Bec's friends. The feeling surprised him having never really felt like he belonged much of anywhere before. Actually things were going pretty well he realized. If only he could do something about Sylvie.

CHAPTER XIX

Clay thought about pushing her, dreamed again of making his feelings known to her. These possibilities occupied most of the drive to Philadelphia. At last after three weeks he would see her again. He knew she would be at Mallary's. She had to be.

She was there. Clay couldn't get enough of looking at her, storing her images in his mind. However, as before, the fragility he sensed in her kept him quiet. How ironic, he thought, that the vulnerability that attracted him kept him from revealing his feelings to her. As at their last meeting, Clay played the part of confidant, hearing all the details of her holiday celebrations. She was disappointed that Clay had nothing to report about Bec but accepted the news that he had gone away for the holidays. She seemed happy that he had gone some place warm and sunny. Clay neglected to tell her that Bec had not gone alone.

The next day Bec returned. He was deeply tanned and in even higher spirits than usual.

"It was fantastic, incredible—turquoise water, sun, sun and more sun," Bec went on stringing superlatives together.

"So I take it you had a good time?" Clay joked.

"My only regret is that I don't have enough money to live that way all the time."

"So that's why you came back—to earn a living?"

"Right. Actually all that sun and fun gave me lots of ideas for a new book."

"I'm afraid to ask."

"Don't worry, you'll be typing it soon enough."

"So did Lydia find this paradise as awe-inspiring as you did?"

"Are you kidding? She loved it, didn't want to leave. I thought she was going to start crying when we got on the plane to come back. Anyway, how was your Christmas?"

"About what I expected," Clay groaned.

"That bad?"

"Could have been worse but I was glad to get back here."

The two talked on for a while. Bec wasn't really in the mood to work yet. The glow from his trip hadn't worn off enough for him to return to the day-to-day. Clay was glad to have him back, this closest thing to a close friend he had had in a long time. The atmosphere in the house seemed complete now.

Eventually Clay got back into his routine: typing what Bec had written, walks on the beach, an occasional dinner at Braeden's. Life seemed to be returning to its pre-holiday serenity. Even Marianne reappeared. Clay knew she had to be in the house when he heard Eric Carmen on the stereo one afternoon. He was glad to see her. Her dimpled smile always made him feel better and took his mind off Sylvie at least for a short while. Bec didn't see too much of Lydia for the next few weeks. Clay wasn't sure if it was his choice or hers but Bec made up for it. Marianne appeared at the house more frequently as did others. Clay could usually tell which one by the music that filled the house. If he didn't recognize the music he figured it must be a new girl. Clay didn't really understand the parade of women in and out of the house considering the way Bec seemed to feel about Lydia. However, he never felt comfortable enough to bring the subject up in conversations with Bec.

Even Clay's meetings with Sylvie seemed to have fallen into a routine. He reported on Bec. Then she talked and he listened all the while dreaming of some miracle that would transform him from confidant into lover.

The only ruffle in the calm surface of January came one Wednesday afternoon in mid-month. Clay was just returning from his usual meeting with Sylvie. As he pulled up at the curb in front of the house, Marianne and a young girl perhaps fifteen or sixteen were getting into Bec's car. Bec waved to Clay as he opened the door to get into the driver's seat. Something in the expression on Bec's face told Clay that he was in no mood to stop for conversation.

Inside the house Clay found Pete in the living room drinking a beer.

"What's with Bec?" Clay asked.

"Did you see him?"

"Yeah, but he didn't say anything. He and Marianne and another girl just got in his car and took off. He looked like he was pissed about something."

"He's really bummed out about Marianne's sister, Gina. She's the one you saw out there with them," Pete

babbled on happy to share his inside info with someone. "Bec and Marianne are taking her to have an abortion. Bec didn't really want to do it but Marianne talked
him into it. Gina's only fifteen and Marianne figured it'd
kill their parents if they found out she was pregnant.
Of course, I guess it would kill them if they found out
she's having an abortion. I'm not sure Gina would really
care either way—she's a pretty wild kid. Anyway, Bec
finally agreed to take her. Now he's all upset because
it started him thinking about his daughter."

"Bec has a daughter?" Clay blurted out in spite of
himself.

"Yeah he hardly ever talks about her though," Pete
went on spurred by Clay's interest. "Bec was married—it was a while ago. They had a little girl. Anyway,
when they got divorced his wife took the kid and
moved out west someplace. She said she didn't want
Bec to see her again—thought he'd be a bad role model
or some shit like that. It really tore him up. I guess that's
why he doesn't like to talk about it."

"That's really rough," Clay shook his head.

Pete nodded in agreement.

Bec came in alone late that night. Clay was just
getting ready to go upstairs to bed.

"Rough day?" Clay commented on Bec's appearance.

"Real rough! I guess Pete told you about Marianne's
sister?"

"Yeah, how is she?"

"She'll be okay."

"How about you?"

"Yeah, I'll be all right. Man I'm really beat though—I'm gonna hit the sack. See you tomorrow."

"Yeah, good night."

That night as Clay lay in bed he thought about what Pete had told him. It brought a new angle to Clay's perception of Bec. Somehow he couldn't quite picture Bec as a father. But perhaps the bitter divorce explained Bec's reluctance to make more of a commitment to Lydia.

Despite January's outward routine and calm, the tumult within Clay's mind increased as the month progressed. His obsession with Sylvie grew. At times he wanted to give her up because he was tired of the effort of thinking about her all the time with no real hope of getting closer to her—just so tired. But he knew he couldn't because he realized how empty his life would be without his thoughts of her. He could not imagine going back to a life without her in his mind. At times Clay wondered if the reality of Sylvie could match his imagination or if his desire for her was the type of passion that would be dissipated by the actuality of day-to-day contact. It didn't really matter though, he knew he had to keep on anyway. If only he could tell her about his feelings—or tell someone. At least he provided Sylvie with an outlet for her secret sentiments for Bec. With no one to open up to, Clay felt at times that the burden of his hidden desires for Sylvie might burn a hole through his brain.

On the last Wednesday of January Clay made his usual drive to Philadelphia. The month had been cold but fairly free of precipitation. This morning was a hard-crystal cold one. The sun shone off a brutally blue sky. Clay was ready for the usual meeting with Sylvie—letting her babble while he daydreamed. He was a little early getting to Mallary's so he was surprised to find Sylvie already seated at their table. When she turned her face up to greet him he knew at once something was wrong. Her skin seemed several shades paler than usual and the dark circles under her eyes spoke of a sleepless night crying. A death in the family? Mistreatment at the hands of her husband? These thoughts flashed through Clay's mind as he seated himself across the table from her.

"What's wrong? You look so sad."

"Oh, I know I must look awful."

Clay tried to reassure her but she shook her head. She was obviously having difficulty holding the sobs back. After a moment and a few sips of water, she seemed more composed.

"It's just that I never expected this—I'm just not prepared."

"Not prepared for what?" Clay asked trying to retain his patience. Was her husband perhaps asking for a divorce?

"My husband has taken another job. We're moving to Seattle," she whimpered.

"Seattle?" Clay found that he was not prepared for this either. He sat staring dumbly across the table at her. It felt as if someone had hit him in the back hard and knocked the wind out of him. 'Seattle—my God, that might as well be the other side of the world,' he thought.

"Yes, I can't believe it," she continued lamenting the loss of friends, nearby relatives, her daughter's school, and of course proximity to Bec. Clay simply nodded from time to time. He really didn't know what to say. What the hell was he going to do?

"It just doesn't seem fair that after all these years, now that I know where Billy is and how he's doing that I'm going to have to give it all up again. I'm really going to miss our meetings, having someone to talk to," she sniffled a little but managed to control herself.

"Maybe I could write and let you know what's going on here," Clay suggested grabbing at the only straw he could see.

"No, I thought about that. It would just be too risky. I'm not sure what my husband would do if he saw any of the letters. I'm afraid it's all over. I'll just have to live with that," she said setting her mouth in a firm line as if trying to convince herself. 'Fine,' Clay thought, 'but how do I live with it?'

"Will this be our last meeting then?" Clay hated to ask the question but felt he had no choice.

"No, I'll be able to come one more time next week," she tried to smile. 'At least a small reprieve,' Clay thought.

"Actually I was hoping we could do something a little different next time," her face brightened a bit.

"Yes, what is it?" he asked, his interest piqued.

"Well, I'll have a little more time than usual next Wednesday afternoon. I thought maybe I could drive down to Trident Beach to meet you. I know this probably sounds silly, but I'd like to see Billy's house—I don't mean the inside of it or anything. I'd just like to drive by—just to see where he lives so I can have that in my mind after I leave. What do you think?" she asked hopefully.

"Well, yes, I don't see why not," at this point Clay would have agreed to meet her on the other side of the moon. Anything—just for another chance to see her.

The next week seemed at once too long and too short for Clay. The possibilities tumbled over and over in his mind, warring with each other for dominance. If he revealed his feelings to Sylvie, was there any likelihood that she might stay. Almost certainly not. What if he followed her to Seattle—tried to set up a new life for himself there. He tried to imagine what that kind of existence might be like. He pictured himself hiding in doorways and behind newspapers trying to catch a glimpse of her. That was if he could even find her at all. Or perhaps he could do as Sylvie had done with her feelings for Bec. Somehow keeping that secret passion in check—not trying to ignore nor extinguish it, for that would be impossible—but some way holding it at bay in the background while carrying on the semblance of a normal life.

Then there was the matter of the life Clay had made for himself in Trident Beach. He had grown to like the town, to truly feel comfortable, at home in this place by the Atlantic. He liked Bec, most of Bec's friends, his job, this new feeling of belonging someplace. He wanted to hold onto the things he had found in Trident Beach. But how could they compete with his need for Sylvie? For a week these thoughts and many more rushed in and out of Clay's mind. They were still shoving each other around when it came time for his last meeting with

Sylvie. He didn't know what to do. He guessed he'd just have to see how she seemed, look for an opening and pray for divine intervention.

CHAPTER XX

They met on the boardwalk near the center of town in front of a fudge shop closed for the winter. Sylvie was bundled up against the sharp wind off the water. She seemed much more serene, in control than at their last meeting. Apparently she had managed to come to terms with her imminent departure and accepted it. They exchanged greetings and walked quickly to Clay's car.

Clay knew he was taking a big chance. What if Bec or one of his friends saw them and asked questions? How would Clay explain? However, he felt he had no choice but to grant Sylvie's request to see Bec's house. Clay drove around the block and approached the house from the south, stopping on the opposite side of the street. Luckily there were no cars in front of the house. Clay could only hope that Bec would not return too soon.

Sylvie sat quietly in the car drinking in the scene, storing it in her memory. After a few moments she smiled sadly. "Okay, that's enough, we can go now." She glanced back over her shoulder lingeringly as they pulled away down the street. Clay was immensely relieved—but what now? Sylvie said she wanted to go back to the boardwalk to see the Atlantic for a last time before moving to the West Coast. They stood at the railing looking out to sea for a moment, then she turned to face Clay. She told him how much she would miss their meetings and having someone to talk to about Billy Becton. And she tried to explain how she had come to accept this turn of fate.

"What more could anyone ask than to know that the one they love is safe and happy?" she smiled but her eyes pleaded. Too much had been given away, they begged for the secret to be kept. Clay understood and nodded. He wanted to grab her, to hold her tightly, tightly enough to squeeze this caring for Bec from her. He wanted to burst into great sobs and tell her that he did understand now—that he understood it all. But instead, he simply took the small, gloved hand she extended and shook it lightly, wishing her good fortune in her new world. He watched her walk off down the boardwalk. When she was out of sight he turned to the East—light blue, dark blue, foam and tears.

Clay spent the next few days kicking himself. How could he have been such a coward? How could he have just stood there and watched her walk away, walk out of his life? After this self-directed anger ran its course the realization set in. There would be no more Wednesday meetings. Now even the slimmest chance of building a relationship was gone. No more Sylvie. He felt empty, bereft. Before, his daydreams had at least been punctuated by the actuality of seeing her once a week. Now he was left with nothing but his thoughts of Sylvie which in her absence seemed to multiply instead of fading. He hated himself for letting her go but knew he couldn't have done otherwise.

Clay tried to hide what was going on inside his head. He forced himself to follow his usual routine but when he no longer needed Wednesdays off, Bec figured something was up.

"Why don't you come to the Westside with us tonight?" Bec suggested as they finished working for the day.

"I don't know—maybe," Clay answered noncommittally. Until now he had avoided going to the Westside with Bec and his friends. He had never been much for the bar scene and he figured this would just be some local joint populated by guys like Arnie with built-in chips on their shoulders.

"Come on—who knows, you might get lucky. It is Valentine's Day after all," Bec laughed.

"Jeez, is it? Hell, why not?" Clay threw up his hands in mock surrender. He had forgotten all about its being Valentine's Day but figured he didn't need to be alone on this of all nights.

Bec, Michael, Pete, Arnie and Clay arrived at the Westside a little after eight. Clay was amazed. He had expected a tiny, dark hole-in-the-wall. As he discovered, the Westside was actually a very small restaurant with a very large, rectangular bar in the middle. It appeared open, almost well-lighted by bar standards. It even seemed clean in a dark, shiny sort of way. Slick was the word that kept coming to mind. Clay was truly surprised, not just because it was a nice place but because it was so different from what he had expected. It even seemed quieter than most bars. A few small pink and red hearts suspended from the ceiling were the only acknowledgement of the holiday. Clay was also surprised at this but grateful. The five chose stools around one of the corners of the bar. The bartender, a heavy-set man in his fifties with a bushy shock of white hair nodded to them.

"Tim, this is Clay—he's kind of new around here," Bec said by way of introduction.

"Glad to meet you," the bartender said with no change of expression. "So what'll you boys have tonight?"

After a while the place began to fill up a bit more, but it still wasn't the rowdy crowd scene that Clay had anticipated. After a few beers, Arnie drifted off toward the jukebox and Michael toward a couple of blondes at the far end of the bar. It seemed Bec didn't have to move, the women came to him. As Bec, Pete and Clay sat at the bar talking several girls stopped by to exchange a few words with Bec. Some he seemed to know, some he didn't.

Finally around eleven, Pete said he was ready to call it a night. As they had all ridden to the Westside in Pete's car Clay decided to leave with him. Bec, Michael and Arnie all seemed quite capable and willing to find other ways of getting home. Clay really hadn't tried to meet anyone that night. That was okay, he hadn't expected to. At least it was one evening he hadn't had to spend dwelling on his loss of Sylvie.

Late that night Clay heard movement in the living room below him then muffled laughter. Van Morrison began to play on the stereo. Must be the tall blonde, Clay thought. As he drifted off to sleep he wondered why Bec wasn't spending this holiday for lovers with Lydia.

CHAPTER XXI

The next morning was bitterly cold. The brutal wind came in strong gusts and ridges of frozen foam on the beach showed where the waves had broken. Clay didn't care. He went out and walked along the sand as long as he could stand it. On his way back from the beach he ran into Bernard, the old house painter who lived down the block from Bec. The old man was trying to start his car. It was an ancient cream-colored station wagon the back of which was crammed full of old paint cans, brushes and well-used drop cloths. Lifting the hood Bernard poured something from a small flask into the car's radiator then proceeded to take a little swig from the same flask himself. 'Jeez, I thought they only did that in old movies,' Clay laughed to himself.

It was Saturday. Clay had no reason to work today as he no longer needed Wednesdays off. He tried to fill the day reading, going to a movie, wandering around town. He kept trying to push Sylvie from his thoughts but she wouldn't go. When Clay arrived back at the house after an early supper he found Bec in the midst of organizing an impromptu party.

"Clay, just the man I've been looking for!" Bec shouted across the living room. "How about going on a beer run with Pete? When you get back I've got a surprise for you," he grinned.

"A surprise?" Clay asked warily.

"Yeah, there's this girl I want you to meet."

"Another Judy Kamasutra?"

"No, nothing like that," Bec smiled. "Her name's Janny. I've known her for a long time. Her brother's an old friend of mine. She's a good kid."

"Have you ever gone out with her?" Clay asked on impulse.

"No, she's too smart for that," Bec laughed.

"I'm really not much for blind dates," Clay winced.

"Come on, man. The hand of fate needs a little slap on the wrist every now and then."

"Okay, okay," Clay finally conceded.

Clay tried to pump Pete for information on their way to get the beer. Unfortunately Pete didn't know much about this Janny. He knew her older brother who had since moved to New England. He had seen her around, that was about it. Clay figured at most it might be another one-night excursion like Judy Camasara. He wasn't sure he was up to that or if he even wanted it. All he really wanted was Sylvie.

The house was beginning to fill with people, noise and smoke by the time they returned. Bec motioned Clay to the far end of the living room. Over the growing din he introduced Clay to the girl standing beside him.

"Clay, this is Janny Roe, the girl I was telling you about."

"Janny, this is Clay Trinian. He's a good man."

She extended her hand somewhat formally for Clay to shake. She was about five-six or seven, not exactly skinny but very slim. Blue-gray eyes, thick sandy-colored hair. She certainly wasn't beautiful but she was pretty enough in a quiet sort of way. After a few moments, Bec left Clay and Janny to their own devices. She seemed so reserved, Clay wondered why she had agreed to this date with a stranger. He felt obliged to try carrying on a conversation with her but it was difficult as the decibel level continued to rise. What he really wanted was to get out of the smoky, noisy room. Finally, he suggested they go for a walk on the beach fully expecting Janny to decline because of the cold. He was surprised when she jumped at the chance. As it turned out she had even less love for loud parties than Clay.

It was a cold night but the wind had calmed making a walk at the water's edge more bearable. The stars were sharp and brittle against the stark black sky. Clay had feared that Janny might complain about the cold. On the contrary, she seemed to come to life when they hit the fresh air. Away from the oppressive noise and smoke she became more animated even friendly. After a walk on the beach Clay suggested they go somewhere for a cup of coffee rather than return to the chaos at Bec's place. She agreed without hesitation.

Clay had not expected much from this evening but he found he liked Janny in spite of himself. They chose Mabee's, the doughnut shop in the middle of town on Twelfth Street between Brigantine Avenue and James Street. It was the one where someone always seemed to be playing "Born on the Bayou" on the jukebox.

"Bec tells me you're working for him," she began.

"Yes, I'm doing some typing and editing for him. I can tell by the look on your face that you're familiar with Bec's work," Clay smiled.

"You're right," Janny laughed. "It's not really my thing but to each his own I suppose."

"So, what do you do with yourself when you're not out on exciting blind dates like this one?"

"I work as a waitress over at The Camelot. Do you know where that is—on Meridien near The Greens?"

"Yeah, I think I've heard of it."

"You'll have to stop in sometime. The food's pretty good. Anyway, I work there and I go to school, sort of."

"Sort of?"

"Well, I just take a couple courses each semester at the community college. At this rate it will probably take me forever to finish but I guess I'll get my degree eventually."

"That must keep you pretty busy," Clay remarked.

"Yeah, it does. I guess that's why I let Bec talk me into meeting you," Janny smiled a little sheepishly. "You know, all work and no play..."

"Fair enough," Clay returned her smile.

"So, you know about me, what about you—or have you always been in the dirty book business?"

"No," Clay laughed. "I tried college for a couple years but it didn't work out. Since then I've done a little of a lot of things."

"I'll bet you read a lot, don't you?" Janny said suddenly.

"Yeah, how'd you know that?" Clay asked surprised. "Do I look like the typical bookworm or something?"

"No, it's not that. I can usually tell, that's all. I think it's really important for people to read a lot."

"Don't tell me, you're a lit. major."

"Guilty," she laughed. "I hope someday I'll be able to teach. What I'd really like to do is teach at college level but that's a long way off."

"A noble goal."

"Yeah, right."

"No, I'm serious," Clay assured her. He checked his watch when he noticed they were trying to close the doughnut shop. "I didn't realize it was so late."

"Gosh, neither did I. Is it really one?"

"'Fraid so."

"I guess I really ought to be getting home. Can you drop me off? It's on your way back to Bec's."

"Sure, be glad to."

It turned out Janny lived only a few blocks north of Bec's house. She was renting out the first floor apartment of a house on the beach. Clay walked her to the front door. They exchanged a friendly goodnight kiss. It was enough to tell him that she had enjoyed herself but that she didn't want anything more from him that night.

The party was winding down by the time Clay returned to Bec's house but there were still enough people for him to slip upstairs unnoticed. He read for a while until the noise downstairs lessened. It had been an enjoyable evening. Janny seemed okay. At least she hadn't asked what his sign was. Maybe he'd give her a call sometime, he thought as he drifted off to sleep.

Clay spent most of the next day, Sunday, out and didn't see Bec again until Monday morning when he came into the writing room.

"So, what'd you think of Janny?" Bec inquired.

"She's okay," Clay answered noncommittally.

"Jeez, what enthusiasm."

"Yeah, she's nice. I had a good time. Okay?"

"So are you going to see her again?"

"I don't know, I might."

"Such passion!"

"Come on, gimme a break, I just met her."

"Okay, okay—let's get to work."

CHAPTER XXII

The next few days passed fairly routinely. At midweek Clay tried to concentrate on his work telling himself that Wednesday was just another day. He walked along the beach even when the cold wind made his face smart and his eyes run. It always seemed to raise his spirits despite the weather. He found himself looking forward to warmer temperatures when he would be able to go out into the water he had spent so much time staring at during the past few months. When he had first arrived at Bec's in mid-September there had still been a few people going swimming in the ocean. He had been tempted to go in then but had felt too self-conscious, too unfamiliar with it. Now he felt ready. He looked out over the water thinking what it would be like and thinking about Sylvie.

On Friday Bec left at noon for New York City to see Lydia. Clay typed on for a while calling it quits around three. It was a somber, rainy day but he felt like getting out for a bit anyway. As he had some books due he decided to pay a visit to the public library at the north end of town. It seemed like a good afternoon to spend there. As Clay passed the checkout desk he ran into

Janny on her way out. The two exchanged whispered greetings.

"Listen, I know it's awfully short notice but would you like to go out to dinner tonight or something?" Clay wasn't sure what had made him act so impulsively.

"I can't, I have to work tonight," Janny looked genuinely disappointed.

"What time do you get off?"

"Around ten."

"Well, we could go out for a late bite to eat then," Clay suggested.

"Okay, that sounds great," Janny smiled.

Clay spent the rest of the afternoon in a corner of the library reading, watching the rain through the long, narrow windows and thinking about Janny and about Sylvie. That night Janny introduced Clay to Regent's, a small pizzeria at the south edge of town. As advertised it was truly the best pizza Clay had ever tasted. They talked and joked, Clay realizing how good it felt to laugh and more, to make someone else laugh. He asked Janny if she wanted to go back to Bec's with him for a while. She declined. Unlike most of the girls Clay had met in Trident Beach who seemed interested only in getting to know Bec better, Janny on the contrary seemed only to tolerate Bec and his friends. She had no desire to get closer to them or to spend more time with them. Clay was somewhat surprised when she suggested they go back to her rental on Ocean Boulevard.

"Well, this is it," she announced turning on the lights.

"Hey, this is a nice place. Right on the beach, too."

"I know. I'd never be able to afford it during the summer. Thank God for off-season rates."

"What's it like here during the summer?"

"Well, it's hotter for one thing," Janny joked.

"Yeah, I kind of figured that," Clay laughed. "Really, though—tell me about it."

"I don't know. I suppose it's like a lot of shore towns in some ways. But it always seems, at least to me, that even at the height of the summer, no matter how crowded it gets, there's something different about it. Like it has its own special feeling. Does that make any sense?"

"Yes, yes it does. I'm looking forward to experiencing it."

They settled in front of a late movie on television. It felt so comfortable, so natural for Clay being there with her. Had he known her for only a week? It seemed natural, too, when he leaned over and kissed her. But he could tell that she still wasn't ready for anything more from him. She was cautious. That was okay.

Clay saw Janny again on Sunday afternoon before she had to go to work. They ran up and down on the beach in the cold. Then they took a drive to Avalon and Stone Harbor mostly just for something to do and to escape from the biting wind for a while. Here Clay was most impressed by the closed-in feeling afforded by the huge, dense, twisted bayberry thickets shaped by wind and the will to survive.

Clay found himself looking forward to Monday and Tuesday, Janny's nights off from the restaurant. On Monday night she cooked dinner for him. On Tuesday night Clay cooked for her. It was a pleasure for him. Although

Janny's kitchen was small it was better-equipped than the one at Bec's house. It didn't seem to bother her at all that Clay was much the better cook. He was very thankful for that as it had caused problems for him with some women in the past.

"That was a great dinner," Janny thanked Clay as they cleared the table. "Just leave the dishes—I'll take care of them later."

"You sure?"

"Yeah, come on, there's supposed to be a good movie on at nine," she answered taking her cup of coffee into the living room. As it turned out, the movie was not on.

"How about some music?" Clay suggested.

"Is the radio okay?"

"Sure. Let's see..." Clay turned on the radio. Loud rock and roll blared out. He turned the dial until he found a mellower station. "Ah, that's better. Would you care to dance?" he asked with mock formality.

"Sure, why not?' she laughed.

They danced around the linoleum floor of the living and dining rooms, kicking up throw rugs in their wake. It felt good to hold her in his arms, to hold her body close against his. There was a warm willingness that Clay had not sensed before. Finally they stood swaying in one spot in the middle of the room. Janny's arms encircled Clay's neck. She rubbed the back of his head gently, brushed his cheek with her fingertips. He kissed her forehead, her lips and tilted her head back to kiss her neck just where it disappeared into her shirt.

"Umm, that's nice," she whispered.

"Umm-humm," he kissed her again. She was smiling, nodding her head in answer to his unvoiced question. The music droned on in the background as they danced slowly down the hall to Janny's bedroom.

Clay got back to Bec's house the next morning just as Bec was crossing the hallway into the writing room.

"Well, aren't we out early this morning or is it very late?" Bec lifted his coffee cup as if toasting Clay.

Clay simply smiled, "Let's get to work." He was glad Bec didn't press him for details of the night before. Clay felt good about it, better than he would have imagined. Janny was open and frank and as guileless in sex as she was in conversation. Clay sensed she didn't feel the need to play the petty games that had turned him off to some women. She was so easy to talk to, to be with.

Clay didn't see much of Janny for the next couple days. She was busy with classes, studying and working. He saw her Saturday before she had to go to The Camelot. They spent the long, drizzly afternoon at her place watching old movies and making love. On Sunday Janny surprised Clay by showing up at Bec's house.

"I saw your car out front and took a chance that you might be here," she smiled. "I hope you don't mind. I thought you might like to go out for Sunday brunch."

"Sure, that sounds great, let me get my jacket. Why don't you come up and see my room while you're here."

"So this is it," Janny said surveying the room.

"Yeah, there's not much to it but it's really all I need."

"Nice windows," Janny noticed the room's one truly admirable feature.

Arnie came through the front door just as Clay and Janny reached the bottom of the stairs.

"Jeez, you two can't get enough of each other can you? In the middle of the day no less," Arnie leered.

Janny hurried out the front door without comment.

"Don't let him get to you," Clay tried to soothe her.

"He's just such an asshole," Janny complained.

"He is kind of an idiot sometimes."

"He's an asshole," Janny maintained.

"Yeah, well, I always figured that an asshole was just a malicious idiot."

Janny smiled. "Okay, I guess I'm overreacting. Arnie's just always affected me that way."

"That's understandable. Let's just forget about him, okay?"

"Okay," Janny agreed but Clay noticed that in the future she was reluctant to visit Bec's house again.

Clay spent more and more time with Janny. Almost without his noticing, she had become a part of his life. She was everything he had always thought he wanted in a woman. She was smart, strong, honest. He felt a growing fondness for Janny. It wasn't the deep hunger he held for Sylvie but perhaps it might be enough. It was all so easy with Janny, so damn easy.

All the while, even when he was making love to Janny, Clay never felt that he was betraying his memories of Sylvie. In fact, instead of fading as his feelings for Janny grew, these thoughts of Sylvie seemed to maintain a life of their own. They lay hidden but alive, like some deep sore festering below after the surface has healed over. Clay's feelings for Janny and Sylvie seemed to be growing on parallel tracks. His relationship with Janny was like breathing fresh, clean air while his feelings for Sylvie were recurring, enduring like malaria. Perhaps Sylvie had been right—perhaps it was possible to love two people at the same time. There seemed to be room enough in Clay's mind for the two of them, at least for now.

Clay spent more and more time at Janny's apartment. He loved being right on the beach so close to the ocean. He cooked for her, read to her and enjoyed discussing the works she was studying. He marveled at the little tricks she used in blow-drying her hair and watched her do aerobics to Rick Springfield. He knew he'd never be able to hear that album again without thinking of Janny in her lime and hot pink striped leotard. Clay enjoyed the feel of the taut, supple body that the exercises produced. He admired her discipline, her toughness. Unlike most of the women he had known, Janny refused to use her period as an excuse for anything. She barely acknowledged it, as if to do otherwise might have been taken as a sign of weakness.

"You know I think he's wrong," Janny pronounced putting down the book she had been reading.

"Who's wrong?" Clay asked over the top of his own book. Janny showed him her book. "Are you sure? That smacks of heresy," he smiled.

"I'm serious," Janny pleaded returning his smile.

"Okay—so?"

"Well, I think he's wrong about there really only being one time for a woman when it comes to sex—the first time. If there really is only one time, I think it's the last time."

"I'm afraid I can't agree or disagree, not being a woman," Clay smiled and reached over to kiss her hand.

"You know I love you, don't you?" Janny whispered. It was true she had let him into her body, into her mind—that was easy—but she had waited until she felt the time was right to let him into her heart. She was a smart girl.

"I love you, too," Clay brushed the hair back from her face and kissed her cheek. He did love Janny, in a comfortable, cozy sort of way.

CHAPTER XXIII

At five o'clock Clay dropped Janny off at work and headed back to Bec's house. He hadn't really expected Bec to be back from New York this early so he was surprised to see the green Fiat at the curb. From the other vehicles Clay could see that Pete and Arnie were there, also.

Clay entered the living room to find Arnie in his usual position, half-drunk sprawled in the most comfortable armchair, a beer in one hand, a cigarette in the other. Not surprisingly he was grumbling about something under his breath. "I can't get anything worthwhile on that damn radio," he growled. "What ever happened to the good old days—Mars Bonfire, King Crimson—whatever happened to them?" he asked belligerently.

"Time marches on, Arnie," Pete, perched on the arm of another chair responded philosophically.

"No lie," Arnie murmured grimly.

"Come on, let's watch this movie before Arnie starts telling his stories about Jersey Devil encounters," Pete seemed to be urging Bec. Bec pacing between the middle of the room and the doorway to the kitchen looked restless and somewhat hollow-eyed. They all barely acknowledged Clay's greeting.

"No, you go ahead and watch it, Pete," Bec mumbled still pacing.

"Come on, it's supposed to be really good—a true-to-life story," Pete seemed uncharacteristically insistent.

"Sorry, I'm just not in the mood for poignancy," Bec shot back with a touch of bitterness.

Clay felt as if he had walked in on a rehearsal for a play, Bec and Pete taking parts in opposition to their usual roles. Only Arnie seemed in character as his normal, unpleasant self.

"I'm going out for a walk," Bec announced. "Alone!" he added quickly as if afraid someone might try to join him.

"Yeah, I guess I'd better be getting home to the old lady," Arnie slowly lifted himself out of the armchair and headed for the front door. In the silence left behind Clay turned to Pete for an explanation. As always, Pete was more than willing to share whatever he knew.

"Bec's really bummed out," Pete volunteered. "I thought maybe I could get him interested in a movie—take his mind off things for a while."

"So what's going on?" Clay asked.

"It's Lydia."

"What? Did something happen to her?"

"I guess you could say that," Pete smiled sarcastically. "She got married to some other guy. Bec's pretty broken up about it."

"Jeez, I guess that would be kind of a shock. He didn't know anything about it beforehand?"

"Didn't have a clue," Pete shook his head. "Look, I've got to get home. Maybe you can talk to Bec when he gets back, try and cheer him up or something."

"Sure, I'll see what I can do."

Clay fixed enough supper for two thinking Bec might reappear at any moment. He finally ended up putting Bec's plate in the refrigerator. After spending the evening reading and watching television Clay gave up at midnight and went upstairs to bed. Any talk with Bec would have to wait until morning.

Monday morning. Clay got up at his usual time. He hadn't heard Bec come in during the night. Perhaps he hadn't come in at all. The house seemed quiet and empty as Clay sat in the kitchen eating breakfast. He thought about Bec. Had he really cared that much for Lydia? Clay wondered. Had he really been that serious about her? Clay went to work as usual typing in the writing room. Around ten he heard a car door close and looked out the front window to see Bec coming up the walk and Marianne driving away.

"Sign of a good employee," Bec poked his head in at the doorway to the writing room. "Working away while the boss is absent." Bec sounded more like his usual carefree self but Clay noticed he still had the look of one who hadn't slept well for several nights.

"There's some coffee in the kitchen," Clay offered looking up from the typewriter.

"Great, I can use some," Bec's voice trailed off down the hallway toward the back of the house. Bec returned with a large mug and some cold potatoes from the dinner plate Clay had put in the refrigerator the night before. "I'll bet these were really good last night, huh?"

"Yeah, I thought you might come back in time for supper."

"I just felt like I had to get out of here for a while. I guess you heard about Lydia?"

"Yeah, I'm sorry man. I don't really know what to say."

"Not much to say."

"You really had no idea?"

"None at all. Some guy she just met through her job. Get this—the guy's older than her father. Maybe the attraction was his wallet—he's giving her a house in the Caribbean and a new car as wedding presents. I guess she just decided he could give her everything I couldn't."

'Including a commitment?' Clay wondered but didn't dare voice the question.

Bec stuck it out for the rest of the day scribbling in his notebooks. Clay could tell from the way he shifted restlessly in his chair and the tapping of his pen on the tabletop that Bec's mind was not really on his work.

"I've had enough of this," Bec announced at five o'clock and went into the living room to telephone Michael. A short time later the silver Mercedes appeared at the curb and Bec and Michael were off to the Westside. Clay hurried to Reno's Market. He had promised to cook for Janny as she had the night off.

"Big test?" he asked from the kitchen.

"Kind of —it's supposed to count for twenty-five per cent of our grade," Janny answered from the living room couch where she was curled up with one of her text books.

Clay thought about her as he made the salad, basted the chicken. He enjoyed these dinners, had come to look forward to the time they spent together. She would lay her studying aside. They'd have a pleasant meal with interesting conversation. Then he would waltz her down the narrow hallway to the bedroom and enjoy her supple, welcoming body. It was so easy, so natural—all so easy. The bell of the kitchen timer rang signaling the need to start cooking the green beans. The flow of Clay's thoughts stopped with the bell and reformed in another direction as he arranged some brown'n'serve rolls on a cookie sheet. Sylvie. Despite Clay's fondness for Janny and the increasing amount of time he spent with her, Sylvie was still there in his thoughts. She seemed to have set up permanent housekeeping in a corner of his mind. As the reality of Clay's relationship with Janny grew so also the unrealizable fantasy of some sort of life with Sylvie gained strength. The bell sounded again. Time for dinner with Janny.

The next morning Clay returned to Bec's house just in time to start working. Bec seemed a little more like his old self, good-naturedly kidding Clay about staying out all night.

"Actually you're lucky you weren't here last night."

"Why? What happened?" Clay asked.

"Well, it was St. Patrick's Day you know."

"Oh, yeah—I'd forgotten."

"Anyway, Arnie considered it a great excuse to get roaring drunk and make a total ass of himself. We had to get him out of the Westside because they were threatening to call the cops. He didn't want to go home and face

Grace so we were going to bring him back here to sober up a little. Halfway here he jumped out of the car and headed for the beach. Anyway, by the time we got him back here he had calmed down to the shouting stage. Luckily he'd gotten over wanting to throw things through windows."

"Jeez! Sounds like a great evening," Clay shook his head. "So what finally happened?"

"Before we could get any coffee into him he passed out on the living room couch. Pete and I carried him home to Grace. Michael was so pissed he took off. Then, to top it all off, when we got Arnie home Grace started yelling at us, blaming us for keeping Arnie out and getting him drunk."

"I'm really sorry I missed all that," Clay said sarcastically.

"Oh, well—I guess Arnie'll never change," Bec said resignedly.

CHAPTER XXIV

The next two weeks passed by fairly uneventfully. Clay and Bec spent weekdays in the writing room as usual. Bec seemed to be gradually getting over the shock of Lydia's marriage. He was seeing more of Marianne though not exclusively. Clay went on typing, seeing Janny, thinking of Sylvie and wondering about the nature of split -personalities. Perhaps, he thought, things would continue on like this forever.

Of course they didn't. The calm was broken on the last Sunday of March. Clay returned to Bec's around six after dropping Janny off at work. From the blue Chevrolet and red truck out front he expected to find Pete and Arnie inside. What he hadn't anticipated was the tense scene that greeted him upon entering the house.

Pete stood in a corner behind a chair as if using the piece of furniture to separate himself from what was taking place in the center of the room. Clay froze at the entrance to the living room. Bec and Arnie stood shouting at each other in the middle of the room. Muscles tensed, they looked for all the world as if they might come to blows at any moment. Bec had always taken Arnie's habitual unpleasantness and occasional drunken outbursts in stride. Clay couldn't imagine what might have caused this scene.

"Since when are you such a moralist?" Arnie yelled. "You would have done the same thing if you'd been in my place," he added defensively. "I'm telling you—she kept coming on to me."

"She's only fifteen!"

"Yeah, well, she doesn't act fifteen!" Arnie leered.

"Jesus-fucking-Christ, Arnie!" Bec's voice rang with an anger Clay would not have thought him capable of. "You really don't get it do you, Arnie? You've really gone too far this time."

"Fuck you!" Arnie shouted and turned quickly to leave kicking a chair in angry frustration on his way out. Clay swiftly sidestepped to avoid the same fate as the chair. Within seconds Bec was out the door, too. Clay heard their two vehicles take off in opposite directions. As usual he turned to Pete for answers.

Pete was still standing in the corner holding onto the back of a chair. He was visibly shaken by what he had just witnessed. For once, he even seemed a bit reluctant to share what he knew. After a few minutes though he relaxed and the words started to flow.

"I've never seen anything like it," Pete began. "Sure they've gotten a little pissed off at each other over the years but never anything like this. I just don't know what's going to happen. I've never seen Bec so angry. I'm not sure he'll ever forgive Arnie."

"Forgive him for what?" Clay was trying to be patient but the suspense was beginning to get to him.

"Well, it all started this afternoon. Arnie came over to watch the ball game. He was already a little bit drunk. He and Grace had another fight. They were supposed to go over to her parents' house for dinner and Arnie didn't want to go. So I guess he decided he'd sort of hide out here for the rest of the day. Anyway, he kept downing the beers all afternoon—even more than usual. By the time the game was over he was really sloppy drunk.

"So Bec got mad at Arnie for being drunk?" Clay interjected hoping to move the narrative along.

"No, nothing like that—you know Arnie—he's always getting drunk. No, the trouble began when Arnie started running his mouth about Marianne's younger sister. You remember—the one I told you about when Bec helped get her an abortion. Anyway, Arnie started bragging about how Gina was always coming on to him, begging him to screw her when she was over there babysitting his kids. Well, Bec was only half paying attention until Arnie let it slip that he actually had done her a few times. Bec ran across the room and jerked Arnie up out of his chair. I swear to God, I thought Bec was going to kill him. If you'd seen the look in his eyes." This had no doubt accounted for Pete's retreat to the corner of the room, Clay thought.

Pete took a long swallow of beer and continued. "I guess Bec figured that Arnie could have been the father of the kid he helped Gina get rid of. Bec told Arnie he should have known better—that there was no excuse no matter how much she came on to him. And I guess you heard the rest. I just don't know what's going to happen now. They've been friends for so long—but this..." Pete's voice trailed off.

"Yeah, I don't know—that's pretty heavy," Clay said thoughtfully. He noticed that Pete offered no judgments of his own regarding Arnie's behavior. Clay guessed that Pete had been too shocked to take any role but that of observer. Clay and Pete sat silently for a while staring at the bottles in front of them. Finally Pete glanced at his watch.

"Jeez, I didn't know it was so late. I gotta get home. Polly'll have dinner ready. I guess we'll just have to wait and see how things work out between Bec and Arnie."

"Yeah, I guess so–see you later," Clay waved him out the front door. Clay stayed up watching television for a while thinking Bec might want to talk when he came back. But at midnight Clay gave up and climbed the quiet stairs in the empty house to his room. Around two he heard the muffled sounds of Bec's return in the rooms below. The noise didn't last long. Clay guessed Bec had gone straight to bed.

At quarter past three, Clay was awakened again. This time by the insistent ringing of the phone in the hall below. He waited for Bec to answer it but it just kept ringing. Reluctantly Clay trudged to the bottom of the stairs just in time to see Bec emerge sleepily from his room.

"I'll get it," Bec waved a hand drowsily toward Clay.

A little more awake now, it dawned on Clay that the phone had rung an inordinately long time. The thought crossed his mind that it might be Arnie, drunk and wanting to apologize. But it wasn't.

"Calm down, calm down, Grace, I can't understand what you're saying." Clay could hear the shrill, incoherent voice coming from the phone as Bec held the receiver away from his ear. "Okay, okay—it's all right, Grace—where is he now? It's okay—I'll be there as soon as I can—I'm leaving right now." Bec was fully awake now. "That was Grace—oh, God—Arnie's been in an accident—sounds bad—I've got to get over there—got to get dressed. Clay, do me a favor, call Michael and tell him to meet me over there, will you?"

"Sure—where?"

"Oh, right—Atlantic Memorial Hospital—Michael knows where it is –emergency room."

"Okay, good luck," Clay offered as Bec ran down the walk to his car. He didn't know what else to say.

Clay called Michael who answered on the second ring and seemed not to have been asleep. After relaying Bec's message Clay thought about taking his own car and joining them at the hospital. He decided against it. For one thing, he had no idea where the hospital was. Besides he hated hospitals and figured he couldn't be of much help anyway. He didn't really feel like going back to bed so he sat in the living room and read for a while.

Clay didn't realize he had drifted off to sleep until he was awakened by the sound of the front door opening. A very haggard-looking Bec walked slowly into the living room and dropped into the nearest chair. Michael, seeming even more somber than usual, followed. Clay looked from one to the other but was afraid to voice a question. Finally Bec spoke in a low, emotionless tone.

"Arnie's dead."

Clay opened his mouth but nothing came out.

"He ran his truck off the road into a tree on Baybridge Road," Michael stated matter-of-factly.

"What the hell was he doing out on Baybridge Road in the middle of the night?" a voice asked from the hallway. Clay guessed that Pete must have been called from the hospital. "Well, what was he doing out there?" Pete reiterated the question as though it really had some bearing on Arnie's senseless death—as if answered correctly perhaps it could bring Arnie back.

"No one seems to know, Pete. No one seems to know why he was out there," Michael answered patiently, kindly as if speaking to a small child. Pete crumpled into the chair next to Clay's. As Bec and Pete sat dazed, Michael filled in some of the details, as much to clarify things for himself Clay guessed as for anyone else's benefit.

Apparently Arnie had continued drinking after he left Bec's the evening before. No one knew where he had spent the intervening hours before the crash. Around two-thirty a passing motorist had seen the truck smashed against a tree and found Arnie inside unconscious. It was uncertain how long he had been there. He had been taken to the hospital, his wife notified. Then Grace, hysterical, had called Bec. Arnie died just before Bec and Michael reached the hospital. He had never regained consciousness.

After a while Bec rose silently and walked off toward his bedroom. Pete mumbled something about having to get home and get ready for work. Michael said he would talk to Grace about making the arrangements. Clay was left alone again in the empty living room.

Later that morning Clay went to work as usual in the writing room. He figured if the typing bothered Bec he'd let him know. Bec finally left his bedroom around noon. Waving away Clay's offer of a sandwich he went out but Clay noticed he didn't take his car. When he returned around six, Bec seemed truly spent, physically as well as emotionally. He said he'd been walking or running all afternoon but it didn't seem to help much. He didn't refuse this time when Clay offered to fix him something to eat. He just sat docilely at the kitchen table waiting. When the food was ready the two sat and ate in silence.

***

The day of the funeral dawned bright and cloudless. The early morning air was fresh and salty and unusually warm for early April. A perfect day but Clay seemed the only one who noticed. He took a long walk on the beach just after sunrise. He had only been to a few funerals, never anyone close, and he wished he could avoid this one. He figured he ought to be there though for Bec's sake anyway. In the few days since Arnie's death Bec hadn't set foot in the writing room. He'd spent most of his time alone in his bedroom or out wandering around on the beach. Clay knew Bec felt guilty because of the argument he'd had with Arnie—perhaps even felt responsible for his death. Clay couldn't get him to talk about it or to talk about much of anything. It would just take time he guessed.

Clay spent Tuesday night with Janny. The only bright spot in an otherwise dreary week. She had offered to attend the funeral with Clay but he hadn't seen any point in putting her through that. She hadn't known Arnie very well and hadn't liked him at all.

Clay had hoped for a quick funeral service but it seemed to drag on forever. They followed the coffin to the cemetery, something he'd never done before. There was a faint breeze, warm and mild. Grass and small plants were beginning to green under the spring sun. The tableau gathered around the hole in the earth seemed incongruous like a scene from a surrealist painting. Those dark suits and dresses and somber faces didn't seem to belong there in the middle of all that sun and warmth and life. This was a new experience for Clay. He had never actually seen a coffin interred before. He noticed how clean and perfect the rectangular shape of the hole was and wondered absently how they got it that way. It was difficult for him to reconcile the image of Arnie as he had known him with this oblong container that was being lowered into the ground. Somehow there was more of a finality to it though than the simple memorial services he had attended in the past.

Finally the service seemed to be concluding. Clay glanced at Bec. Bec had stood silently, broad shoulders hunched, head bowed throughout. He had worn dark glasses against the sun's glare and also, Clay knew, to hide the dark circles beneath his eyes. The mourners were beginning to move away from the graveside when a shrill cry pierced the warm, still air.

"You! It's all your fault!" Everyone turned to see Grace waving her hands in Bec's face. "It's always been you and your friends. He never had time for me and the kids. It's your fault –it's your fault he's dead!" she screamed.

At this point Arnie's widow was subdued by several family members and forcibly led to a waiting car. Throughout the church and graveside services Clay noticed she had been stiff, her jaw rigid, her face unnaturally white. He wished for Bec's sake that she'd been able to hold back that flood of venom at least until he'd be better able to cope with it.

"Do you believe that?" a familiar voice sounded at Clay's side.

"Pete, I didn't see you before."

"Yeah, I got here late—got held up on a job. I always knew Grace was a little over the edge but I can't believe she'd say something like that to Bec. You know he and Michael paid for all this."

"What, you mean the funeral?"

"Yeah, coffin, flowers, plot, everything."

"Does Grace know that?"

"Yeah, I guess she figures they just did it out of guilt or something." Clay wondered if she were right.

Bec and Michael decided to go to Boston for the weekend. Probably just as well Clay thought. Maybe it would take Bec's mind off things. With the house to himself Clay invited Janny over and cooked her an elaborate dinner late Saturday night. It felt good to see her, to touch her and to talk about something other than Arnie and his untimely demise. Clay spent Sunday with Janny, too. They had a late breakfast at Braeden's, read the Sunday paper and took a long walk down the beach in the afternoon. The breeze had turned somewhat sharp but the sun still warmed. They found a little hollow in the dunes away from the wind and sat together staring out at the sea. When the time came, Clay reluctantly dropped her off at work. He didn't want to let her go. It had been a great weekend after such a lousy week. Janny always seemed to make him feel good, comfortable.

As he drifted off to sleep that night Clay thought about Bec and wondered if the trip to Boston had done him any good. He had called to say that he'd be back sometime late tomorrow. Clay hoped that Bec would be in a better frame of mind and ready to get back to work writing. Clay had almost finished typing the backlog of Bec's work. He feared that if Bec didn't start writing again soon they'd both be out of a job.

Clay spent the next morning at the typewriter. Around noon, a call came from Bec's publisher about a deadline. Clay stalled as best he could. Bec and Michael returned late in the afternoon. Clay was alarmed to see that if anything, Bec seemed worse than when he left on Friday. Bec mumbled a hello and headed straight for his bedroom.

"I was hoping he'd be better," Clay couldn't help voicing his concern once Bec was out of earshot.

"Yeah, so was I," Michael said regretfully. "He wasn't doing too bad until we ran into Lydia's sister. I'd forgotten she had moved to Boston. Then it seemed like everything just came crashing down on him all at once.

Lydia, Arnie's death, Arnie and Marianne's sister—he even started talking about his ex-wife and daughter. I've never seen him like this. I don't really know what to do for him." For once, Michael seemed genuinely at a loss. "Keep an eye on him will you?"

"Sure—of course," Clay assured him. "Oh, Michael," Clay caught him as he was turning to leave,"I just remembered—Bec's publisher called today about a deadline."

"Mmm—don't mention it to Bec—he has enough to worry about tonight. I'll talk to him about it tomorrow."

"Okay, good night," Clay closed the front door behind him. It was the first time, he thought, that Michael had let his guard down enough to have a normal one-on-one conversation with him.

CHAPTER XXV

The next few days followed much the same pattern. Bec got up late, skipped breakfast and appeared in the writing room around eleven. But he couldn't or wouldn't concentrate and left after an hour or so for parts unknown, probably the beach. Around seven he would return and sit silently at the kitchen table while Clay fixed dinner. Clay noticed that Bec didn't look quite as haggard and hollow-eyed as he had upon his return from Boston. But still, he had the air of the sleepwalker about him.

Clay tried to enlist Marianne's help in cheering up Bec. She did what she could but Bec didn't seem to respond. In truth, the revelation that Bec's friend had been involved with her sister had driven a wedge between them. In spite of herself, Marianne could not feel quite the same about Bec after that. She seemed uncomfortable in the house perhaps because Arnie had spent so much time there.

Clay saw little of Janny that week. He felt he ought to spend the time with Bec to let him know someone was there even if he wasn't talking. As Michael had said, to keep an eye on him. It worked out all right as Janny had a lot of studying to catch up on. Still, Clay missed her—her voice, her touch.

On Friday evening while Bec was taking a shower Michael motioned Clay into the writing room. "He hasn't been writing has he?" Michael asked with a frown.

"No, not at all."

"I was afraid of that. I talked to his publisher yesterday," Michael ran a hand through his dark, wavy hair.

'Oh, great!' thought Clay. 'This is the part where I get fired because there's nothing left to type.' Expecting the worst, he was amazed by what Michael proposed next.

"Look, I don't know if you'll go for this—I'm not sure I even like the idea. I've talked to Bec and to his publisher, like I said. Anyway, the publisher says as long as he gets something more or less in Bec's style by the end of the month he'll be satisfied. You've been working with Bec for a while now—you know how he writes. Do you think you could fill in for him—just for a while 'til he gets over all this?" Michael looked Clay straight in the eye. Clay couldn't believe he was serious.

"What? Are you joking?" Clay asked incredulously.

"No, I'm not joking," Michael replied a trifle impatiently. "You'd really be doing him a big favor," he added softening a bit.

"I don't know—I guess I could try." Clay didn't really know what else to say. "Bec writes some pretty wild stuff though ya know?"

"I'm sure you can use your imagination if nothing else," Michael said with a sly smile. "We'd better get back into the living room," he added, noting that the shower had stopped running. "I'll tell Bec that it's all set then?"

"Yeah, okay," Clay turned to go upstairs. He needed time to process this unexpected development.

Janny left the next morning to spend a week with her brother in New Hampshire. With nothing but time on his hands Clay thought why wait until Monday?—might as well spend the weekend trying to write. He felt a little self-conscious at first sitting at Bec's table in the writing room. He spoke to Bec about agreeing to Michael's plan. Bec had said impassively, 'that's great' and promptly changed the subject. Clay felt a little more at ease after Bec went out for the day.

Initially he tried writing long-hand as Bec had done but he soon found he did much better typing straight onto the machine and making the necessary changes later. At least Bec had gotten three-quarters of the way through this book. Clay was grateful he hadn't had to start from scratch. If he could just follow Bec's outline, maybe weave in some of the ideas from his notebooks—perhaps he could pull this off after all. Clay's confidence grew as the day progressed. By the end of Saturday he was sure he could do it and by Sunday evening he was actually enjoying himself. He was surprised and thrilled.

On Monday morning Clay got up early. He couldn't wait to start writing. He found he was truly excited at the prospect of working on Bec's book—not just titillated by the subject matter—but enthusiastic. He couldn't remember when he'd felt this eager to do something. Each time he sat down at the typewriter now he was accompanied by a sense of amazement and delight.

Bec seemed to be slowly improving. He wasn't quite as morose though he still showed no signs of wanting to write or to talk at any great length. He spent most of the next week on the beach or wandering around town. The weather was beautiful—the sunny, clean, crisp days of early spring. Clay almost envied him spending so much time outdoors now. In the evenings Bec read or did crossword puzzles which became something of an obsession. He was better but the spark that made him Bec was still missing.

The week passed swiftly for Clay as he became more and more involved in the writing. He thought about Janny's return on Saturday and smiled. It would be good to see her again—to share with her the news of his new job. Clay found he had been thinking more about her and less about Sylvie. This surprised and pleased him. Perhaps he might be cured after all.

On Friday evening Bec went with Michael and Pete to the Westside. As far as Clay knew it was the first time any of them had been there since Arnie's death. Clay stayed at the house alone playing some of Bec's "Steely Dan" albums and thinking about Janny's return the next day. He realized it was the first time the stereo had been used in several weeks.

Clay had dinner ready and waiting for Janny at her place when she returned late Saturday.

"So how was New England?"

"Great! I really liked it up there. I'd like to go back sometime," Janny smiled untwining her arms from around Clay's neck. "So how was your week—is Bec doing any better?"

"Yeah—well, he's coming around slowly I think. But guess what?" Clay couldn't contain himself any longer. "I have a new job!" he blurted out not waiting for a reply.

"Really, a new job?" Janny looked hopeful, "you mean you're not working for Bec anymore?"

"Well, yes I am but not just typing. Now I'm writing—actually writing. Of course it's just 'til Bec gets back in the mood again but I'm really getting a kick out of it."

"You mean you're writing that same porno stuff that Bec does?" she asked obviously disappointed.

"It's not really porn—besides it does take a certain talent ya know," Clay countered defensively hurt that she didn't share his enthusiasm for the new job. But he assured her that it was only a temporary arrangement and joked that he wouldn't expect her to do anything too kinky in the name of research. This smoothed things over and they spent the rest of the evening in each others' arms making up for the week apart. He really had missed her, Clay thought, as he drifted off to sleep, Janny's head resting lightly on his chest.

The next day, Sunday, was a busy one. Michael had decided to throw himself a lavish birthday party. For a generous fee he had enticed Clay into fixing most of the food for the affair. Clay spent the day shopping, chopping, dicing and baking. He enjoyed it but found it didn't provide him with quite the same rush that he experienced when working on Bec's book.

The party was to be held that evening at Michael's. Clay had never seen Michael's house before. He gathered from Pete that this must be quite an occasion as Michael didn't usually invite more than two or three people at a time to his precious place—'The Palace,' Pete had called it. Pete had been right. The house was large for one person especially by beachfront standards. On Surf Road at the northern end of town it was two stories and ultra-modern outside and in. The downstairs was spacious and airy and everywhere echoed the same sense of taste and wealth that Clay had noted in Michael's clothing. The furnishings and artwork in the living room were all of a very modern style. The effect achieved, however, was one of elegant sophistication rather than the blunt, barren scapes Clay had come to associate with most 'modern ' settings. He could see what Pete had meant. Clay couldn't imagine the noisy, smoky parties of Bec's house taking place here.

In truth, it was not a large party that Michael had assembled to celebrate his birthday: Clay, Janny, Bec, Marianne, Pete and his wife, Polly, Michael and a new friend, Simone. Clay guessed that the party was as much for Bec's benefit as anything else. Clay and Janny arrived early to finish the last minute preparations. Clay was awed by the shiny, well-equipped kitchen and wondered if Michael ever used it himself or kept it just for show. Clay put the finishing touches on some stuffed mushroom caps. With a flourish he raised his voice in a broad imitation of 'The French Chef'.

"What the hell's that?" Pete asked drifting in from the living room.

"It's supposed to be Julia Child—where's your sense of 'au courant'?" Michael smiled.

"Kind of sounds more like W.C. Fields with his nuts caught in a vise," Pete commented.

"Yeah, I think you may be right," Clay laughed and noticed that Bec standing in the kitchen doorway laughed,
too. Michael appeared in the doorway behind Bec just
in time to see Clay reach over and give Janny an affec-
tionate peck on the back of the neck.

"Well, if it isn't the Siamese twins—joined at the bed,"
Michael laughed good-naturedly. "Seriously, it looks
like you've done a great job," he added surveying the
trays and dishes laid out on the counter tops waiting to
be served.

The dinner went well. Bec seemed a bit more cheerful. Away from Bec's house Marianne was more relaxed. Janny didn't seem to mind spending the evening
with Bec and his friends perhaps because with Arnie's
death the most obstreperous of the friends was absent.
Michael blew out the candles on the cake Clay had
baked for the occasion. A filmy wisp of white smoke
lingered over the table—the special, unique smell after candles on a birthday cake have been extinguished.
It made Clay think of many other birthdays over the
years. Always that scent of sulfur and cheap wax. He was
brought out of his reverie by Pete raising his glass in a
toast to the birthday boy.

Michael seemed pleased, Clay thought. And why
shouldn't he be? The party was a success. The food had
turned out well, everyone had a good time and perhaps
most importantly, Bec seemed a little better. Clay felt a
bit more at ease around Michael now. Not that the two
of them would ever be close but Clay was beginning to
know what to expect from him. Clay found that Michael
was most cordial to him when it involved doing some-

thing for Bec's benefit. Still Clay sensed there would always be a barrier between Michael and himself and he guessed it might be Michael's jealousy at the friendship that had developed between Clay and Bec. Clay understood the puns and jokes that Michael had flung over the heads of Arnie and Pete, intending them only for Bec's entertainment. He couldn't help but wonder how Michael really felt about Arnie's death—one less friend to claim Bec's attention?

CHAPTER XXVI

Clay went out for a walk on the beach early on Wednesday morning before starting in on the day's writing. It was going well and he was quite pleased with himself. Not just about the writing but about this whole new life he had set up for himself. New friends, Janny, the chance to spend so much time beside the sea. As he ambled along the water's edge, collar turned up against an early, fresh breeze, he thought absently how important Wednesdays had once been to him. How he had longed for each Wednesday to roll around and how he had clung to each moment of the brief meetings with Sylvie. It all seemed so far away now. Turning back toward the house Clay glanced up at the sky. The small, white clouds forming against the pale blue brought to mind his mother's treasured Wedgwood china. It should have seemed a beautiful sight, Clay thought, but there was something a touch eerie in the pale of the sky.

Clay walked the rest of the way back to the house thinking of nothing in particular just enjoying the sweet, morning air. As he closed the front door behind himself he was greeted by a strange fragrance. No—it wasn't altogether strange—there was something familiar about it. While his mind was still busy checking its remembrance files to identify the scent his eyes connected with pale skin and dark hair in the living room. The sensory overload left Clay standing, mouth open, in the middle of the hallway.

"Clay, is that you? Come on in here and meet someone," Bec called from the living room. Clay's feet obediently turned in the direction of Bec's voice but his brain was still trying to assimilate the face he had just seen through the half-open living room door and the smell of hyacinths.

"Clay, this is Sylvie Vallen—ah—Daros now," Bec smiled nodding toward the attractive, young woman with dark hair and large, dark eyes.

"How do you do?' Clay managed in a somewhat stilted, formal tone. By now his mind had changed gears from stunned to racing wildly. Thoughts flew by at a dizzying speed but the overriding motif in all of them was abject fear.

"Sylvie and I used to know each other—way back a long time ago. She heard I was living here and happened to be in the neighborhood and here she is," Bec smiled. Apparently that explanation for Sylvie's presence hadn't seemed in the least strange to him.

"Oh, that's nice—always nice to see old friends," Clay babbled as his mind swam. So she hadn't said anything to Bec about knowing Clay or about how he had originally come to be there. Hell, she acted like she'd never set eyes on him before. Was he going crazy or was this just a very bad dream. Clay felt he had to escape.

"Well, I guess I'll get to work—nice meeting you," Clay said as nonchalantly as possible backing out of the room.

"Okay, see you later," Bec called after him.

Clay sat down in front of the typewriter. He was sweating and he felt like he was going to throw up. What the hell was going on? He couldn't make sense of any of it. After a few minutes it dawned on him that Bec might expect to hear typing sounds coming from the writing room. Clay knew there was no way he could work on the book. Desperately he grabbed a magazine from a nearby table, opened to the leading article and just started typing. He found the automatic action of typing someone else's words—not worrying about their meaning—had a calming effect on him. He was immensely relieved when Bec and Sylvie went out for lunch. He needed time alone to think, to figure out what was going on. Taking his fingers from the keys Clay noticed they were shaking visibly. The feeling lingered of having just awakened from a very disturbing dream.

Still operating mainly on instinct Clay fled to the beach. He knew he didn't want to be in the house if Bec and Sylvie returned there after lunch. He should spend the afternoon working he told himself but he couldn't. He needed some time alone to think, to plan. And besides, there was no way he could concentrate on Bec's book, not now, not today at any rate. Clay paced quickly up and down a small stretch of sand, thought about going back for his car, but rejected it for fear of running into Bec and Sylvie. Instead he turned north and began walking swiftly, purposefully along the water's edge. To his clouded mind The Greens, the residential area at the northern end of town, seemed a haven. Surely Bec and Sylvie would have no reason to go there. He would be safe to walk about and think. He had to get there. Having latched onto this objective for the immediate future Clay felt a little better. He put all his energy toward reaching the neighborhood as if when he got there some miraculous resolution would present itself. He stayed on the beach walking quickly head down until he was well past the center of town. Finally he turned inland to walk the few blocks to where Woodbine Drive split off from Columbus Street. Checking the near empty streets for Bec's car Clay felt like a hunted animal hoping to elude detection.

At last Clay reached The Greens. It had been a long walk and his clothes were sticking to him despite a cool breeze. He relaxed his pace a bit realizing how hard he'd been pushing himself to reach this place. He found no miraculous revelation here, nevertheless, he felt safe for the moment. Although this area of town was largely inhabited year round there weren't many people out on a weekday afternoon in April. He was free to wander from street to street while his mind gradually cleared. He had been right, he thought, when he first saw this part of town. It was a good place to walk, to think away from the distraction of the ocean and insistence of the wind at water's edge. Today Clay found them comforting, these well-kept homes with their tiny, pampered lawns set on narrow, gently-curving streets. Their sense of permanence contrasted with most of the rest of the town. These were not the windswept houses of summer vacationers but the homes of people who had chosen to spend their entire lives close, but not too close, to the sea.

As the shadows of late afternoon began to form Clay knew he would have to head back to Bec's house. In his hurry to escape he had come away without a jacket. Once the sun went down the evenings were still quite cool at this time of year. The physical exertion of walking for several hours had calmed Clay. He felt more peaceful now if nothing else. He walked back through the center of town. He was too tired and hungry to worry about dodging Bec and Sylvie now. As he passed the old movie theater a flash of memory hit him. He was supposed to be taking Janny to a late movie that night. Knowing he couldn't manage it Clay stopped at a pay phone and dialed Janny at the restaurant where she worked. He told her something had come up offering no further explanation. She seemed a little disappointed but understanding. Janny...His feelings for her were so different from the ones he had held for Sylvie.

And what were his feelings for Sylvie? At some point during the long walk Clay's initial fear had dissipated. In its place had come all the obsessive longing and fantasies for Sylvie, all the desires that Clay thought had been safely packed away and relegated to the small corner of his mind now labeled 'Sylvie in Seattle'. Like the hot flow from a fractured volcano the thoughts of her ran into his mind burning new furrows as they went. Clay didn't know why Sylvie had returned, if she would reveal his secret, nor what he would do in that eventuality. By the time he reached Bec's house he was only aware of one need. He knew he had to see Sylvie again.

The stereo was on Clay noticed as he entered the house. It sounded like the Moody Blues. He found Bec and Sylvie sitting on the living room sofa talking and smiling. Clay couldn't help but see that Bec looked the best he had in weeks.

"Clay, we just got back from dinner at Piper's. Too bad you weren't around, you could have gone with us," Bec said in a friendly tone. Clay guessed though from the atmosphere between the two of them that his presence had not been missed. Sylvie smiled. 'Jesus,' the thought struck Clay, 'how could I have hoped to forget her?'

"Great news!" Bec continued. "Sylvie's going to be in town for a while and I've persuaded her to stay with us," he announced happily.

"Oh, that's nice," Clay stammered. Why did he always seem to be at a loss for words in her presence? Politely excusing himself Clay headed for the kitchen to do something about the hunger that had goaded him all the way back from The Greens. What he really wanted was something simple, quick. But he decided to cook some pasta and made an elaborate salad giving him more time to eavesdrop through the open door to the living room. He forced himself to eat slowly despite his by now ravenous hunger. Playing for time, he hoped to overhear something valuable or at least useful. He was rewarded only with reminiscences of adolescence and college life during the sixties. Finally when he could no longer reasonably put it off Clay said his good nights and went upstairs.

Clay stayed awake for a couple hours figuring that eventually they would tire of their stroll down memory lane and Sylvie would come up to one of the empty rooms on the second floor to sleep. Perhaps even the room next to his Clay thought hopefully. Then he would have his chance to talk to her alone. He really wouldn't be able to do anything until he had talked to her. Clay fell asleep waiting.

The physical exertion and emotional stress of the previous day took their due. Clay slept deeply and awakened unusually late the next morning. Opening his eyes he was alarmed to see it was already past ten. Automatically he thought about hurrying down to the writing room to get to work. Then the events of the day before suddenly burst in on his mind like clouds unloading in a downpour. Sylvie. Where was she? Which room was she in? Was she up yet? Clay stuck his head out into the hallway. All was quiet. He thought about trying the door to each room but decided against it. Instead he washed and dressed quickly and went downstairs to the kitchen figuring he'd find out her room number over breakfast. Clay was just putting the coffee on when he was startled by a laugh coming from Bec's bedroom across the hall. What surprised him was the realization that it was not Bec's laugh but a woman's. Bec and Sylvie came across the hall to the kitchen. Bec was wearing only pajama bottoms and his fleur-de-lis tattoo, Sylvie a long silk dressing gown in an intricate paisley print.

"Glad to see you've got the coffee started," Bec smiled sleepily.

"Yeah, I'm afraid I overslept this morning," Clay tried his best to sound natural though the sight of Sylvie emerging from Bec's bedroom in that filmy robe was battering hard at something inside him. "Sylvie and I were talking about old times last night," Bec said stretching. "It brought back a lot of memories, good memories."

Sylvie smiled and nodded her agreement. Clay couldn't help noticing that she looked very happy perhaps even smug sitting there at the kitchen table with Bec. Somehow Clay managed to last until the coffee was ready. Pouring a cup he excused himself to the writing room. 'My God,' he thought once he was alone, why had the idea that Sylvie might spend the night in Bec's room never crossed his mind? But there she had spent it and presumably in Bec's bed as well. Now jealousy jostled in to vie for Clay's attention along with fear and desire. He knew he couldn't leave the house again today. He would just have to find some way of dealing with it. Perhaps the old cliché of plunging oneself into one's work might do it. He felt he had no choice but to try. It was difficult at first but by late afternoon Clay found that by focusing his concentration on writing he was able to crowd Sylvie out of his mind for a while. The thrill he had known previously in writing was replaced by a sense of solace, escape.

Bec and Sylvie went out for an early dinner and then on to the Westside. Clay was left alone at the kitchen table with his questions and his fears. Why was she here? Clay knew the answer to that one was all too obvious. To be with Bec of course. But what about her husband and daughter? Had they moved back here, too, or were they still in Seattle? Had she left her husband and the child as well? And if so, why now? Clay needed answers. He also needed reassurance. It was clear that she had not told Bec about him—about his original mission in

Trident Beach, about knowing him before, about her having hired him. Clay felt a knot in his throat as he remembered taking that envelope of cash from Sylvie. Money for spying on Bec. Would she reveal him? Clay had gotten so used to this new existence that he had almost forgotten he might be skating on very thin ice. He wanted Sylvie, needed her. But he hated the idea that she might jeopardize this bright, new life of his, the novel sense of belonging. Clay had truly come to regard Bec as a friend and he guessed Bec felt the same about him. What would his reaction be if Sylvie told him the truth? Clay tortured himself for a while with these barbs until another sharper one made itself felt.

Janny. What about Janny? He had been so busy thinking about Sylvie and the danger to his new identity. But Janny formed a large part of that new identity. Clay hadn't seen her since Sylvie's sudden appearance. He had only spoken to her briefly on the telephone last night to cancel their date. Had it only been last night? It seemed like much longer, as if Sylvie had been back in his life forever, as if she had never left. Clay tried to focus on Janny's face in his mind, tried to summon up the good feelings of the comfortable love he shared with her. But all that met the senses of his inner life were the pale skin and dark hair, the overpowering scent of hyacinths. The only feeling he seemed capable of was desire—desperate and irrational. Clay fell asleep that night still wrestling with his questions and uncertainties.

Finally the next morning Clay got his chance to talk to Sylvie alone. She and Bec were planning to go to Atlantic City for the day. Before they left Bec had some errands to run. Sylvie decided to stay at the house saying she wanted to make a few phone calls. In reality it turned out she was as eager to talk to Clay as he was to talk to her.

"I was so worried you might say something," she whispered breathlessly after Bec had driven away. Clay was somewhat relieved to see that she had been as fearful of discovery as he.

"No, of course I wouldn't. But why are you here? I mean what happened to Seattle?" Her dark eyes met his, blinked rapidly and she smiled.

"It's so good to be able to talk to someone about this again. I really missed our Wednesday meetings. I thought I was going to be all right in Seattle. I tried, I really did..." her voice trailed off. She seemed to be trying to convince herself as much as Clay. "It just didn't work out. My husband had to spend so much time at his new job and I didn't know anyone," she continued, rationalizing. "And I kept thinking about Billy—Bec—and how you had found him for me after so many years. I just felt I had to come back here and be with him," she smiled as if this were a perfectly logical conclusion.

Clay thought of asking Sylvie about her daughter but decided against it. Instead he asked, "So you're planning on staying in Trident Beach—permanently I mean?"

"Yes, of course," she answered brightly as if it had been a silly question.

"Listen, I hope you'll understand—I'd really appreciate it if you wouldn't say anything to Bec or anyone about how I came to be here. I've kind of gotten used to being here and I'd just as soon leave things as they are," Clay looked at her hopefully.

"Oh, I understand, I won't say a word. And you won't say anything about our Wednesday meetings?"

Clay nodded. "Of course not."

Reassured she went on. "Actually I'm glad you're here. It'll be nice having someone around that I can talk to —you know, really talk to about Bec and everything. You do seem to fit right in here and Bec says you've been a great help to him." That captivating smile again.

At that point, Bec returned and he and Sylvie were off for Atlantic City. Clay turned back to his writing. He felt a little better. Sylvie seemed to have at least as much to lose as he if their previous relationship as detective and client were revealed. But still he felt uneasy. Sylvie's sudden appearance and interjection into Bec's life. Clay couldn't be positive but there seemed something slightly different about Sylvie. Some almost imperceptible change from the woman he had known in Philadelphia. As if her appealing childlike vulnerability had reverted to something even more simple, more elemental. He put it out of his mind as best he could and spent the rest of the day working on Bec's book.

CHAPTER XXVII

The next morning, Saturday, was perfect. The kind of day that should be spent in a town like Trident Beach. Clay decided to spend the weekend with Janny at her place. Escaping from the house he would pretend at least for two days that Sylvie was still in Seattle. Sylvie had made it clear that her attention was focused squarely on Bec. Clay knew he would have to find some way of living with that, of dealing with it on a day-to-day basis. He hoped the best course might be strengthening his own relationship with Janny.

On the way to Janny's house Clay was aware of the increasing activity level in Trident Beach. As spring progressed each weekend brought out more people. He could almost feel the sleepy town stretching, crawling out of its off-season hibernation. Clay was looking forward to summer. He didn't think he'd even mind the crowds too much. It would be a change, a part of the cycle of seasons in this place he had come to think of as home.

Clay opened the door. There in her green and pink leotard was Janny bouncing up and down to the Rick Springfield album again. The music surrounded her and Clay as well as he entered the room. He couldn't help but smile at her healthy exuberance. He took her in his arms and held her close, kissed her glistening neck. She felt like a fresh breeze blowing through the doubts and fears he had been harboring since Sylvie's reappearance. If he could just spend the rest of his life or at least the rest of the weekend like this in Janny's arms—maybe everything would be all right. Maybe.

Clay and Janny spent the weekend as they spent most of their time together—talking, walking, reading, loving in a cozy kind of near-domesticity. But while part of Clay was basking in the refreshing vitality and comfort of Janny's company another part of him was still in the depths. As before it was apparent that Sylvie had no idea of Clay's true feelings for her. Her interest was only in Bec. Clay wondered if he could somehow hide his feelings for Sylvie and continue playing house with Janny. It was possible, as Sylvie had said, to be in love with two people at the same time. Just not very practical, Clay realized. Not very practical at all, he thought, remembering Sylvie's husband and wondering what had become of him.

By the end of the weekend Clay was certain of only one thing. He knew he could never confide in Janny the real reason he had first come to Trident Beach. She was so honest, so open. Even with all her understanding, Clay knew there was no way she could comprehend or forgive such a deception. It pained him that he could not fully return her honesty. Perhaps if he had met Janny first before Sylvie. Perhaps he could have been blissfully happy now instead of stupidly miserable.

Clay returned early to Bec's house on Monday morning. He wanted to get started, make up for time he had lost the previous week when Sylvie's arrival sent him into shock. But as he sat down in front of the typewriter Clay felt perhaps he had returned to the house a little too early. Through the wall separating the writing room from Bec's bedroom Clay could hear low voices, then laughter, then sounds of pleasure. He couldn't make out what they were saying. It didn't matter, he could guess. Clay wondered if they knew he was in the next room. Probably not. Under other circumstances Clay would have politely tiptoed out for a walk on the beach until Bec's guest had left. But this was different. It was Sylvie on the other side of that wall with Bec.

Clay started in on the typewriter keys striking them more forcefully than usual trying to make as much noise as possible. If they knew he was there maybe they'd stop whatever it was they were doing Clay reasoned. As he sat before the typewriter Clay became aware of an unfamiliar feeling creeping over him. It seemed to work its way from loins to chest to brain. The fact that it was a new sensation in itself might have interested Clay had the feeling not been such an unpleasant one. For the first time Clay found himself engulfed by the primeval darkness of sexual jealousy. Furiously he typed on. Anything to avoid thinking about the couple in the next room. Clay was surprised to find that Bec himself seemed to figure little in this emotional scenario. Clay didn't blame Bec, curiously didn't seem to feel any differently about him than he had before. It was just the idea of Sylvie lying with another man so close by—any man—that tormented Clay.

Clay went on typing like a madman until Bec and Sylvie left the house about an hour later. Still burning he channeled his new-found, tumultuous energy into writing. Perhaps he would never again feel the euphoric thrill he had experienced when he first started on Bec's book. Somehow the shock of Sylvie's reappearance had seized that away. But now Clay wrote on, feeling it was something he was meant to do, 'An escape, a vocation, my destiny perhaps?' he thought melodramatically. At any rate it calmed him providing a sturdy vessel to hold the dark feelings that were escaping from within him.

The next two weeks passed by quietly if agonizingly for Clay. Bec was better, almost back to his old self, although he still showed no signs of wanting to return to writing. For this Clay was selfishly grateful. He had finished Bec's book before the deadline and the publisher had been satisfied if not laudatory. Now at Bec's urging Clay was starting on a book of his own under the Becton Delacroix pen-name. The new creative venture was for Clay an island of light in the otherwise black tangle of his emotional life.

Clay had never seen Sylvie happier. He was glad of that just sorry that he was not the reason for it. In a very short time she had managed to insinuate herself deeply into Bec's life. Aided by his emotional vulnerability she became his constant companion. Clay had never known Bec to spend so much time so exclusively with one woman. He guessed that for Bec Sylvie represented a return to a happier, simpler time in his life, before

Arnie's death, before Lydia's rejection, even before his failed attempt at marriage and fatherhood. Clay was glad for Bec, happy that he was healing. But why did it have to be with Sylvie?

Clay managed to keep his feelings for Sylvie hidden, brooding and boiling under a thin crust. How much longer he could keep this up he didn't know. He was still spending time with Janny although his growing sense of guilt was cutting into the comfort and consolation he found there. He knew it wasn't really fair to keep seeing her feeling the way he did about Sylvie. But he didn't want to let go while some possibility persisted in the back of his mind that Sylvie might leave again. Clay knew it was dishonest and cowardly, covering his emotional bases in this way. He just didn't feel strong enough to make any major changes in his life. He would do what he had always done—coast along and see what happened.

CHAPTER XXVIII

On a Tuesday afternoon in mid-May, Clay at the type-writer heard voices coming from Bec's room next door. This time they were not the low, muffled sighs of love-making. Bec's and Sylvie's voices were raised, not in an argument really, but a serious discussion. Clay caught enough while typing to gather that Sylvie was propos-ing some sort of permanent commitment and Bec was predictably declining. After a while he heard Bec close the front door firmly and drive away. Not more than two minutes later Sylvie appeared at the doorway of the writing room.

"I hate to disturb you but I really need to talk to someone," she said hesitantly entering the room. Her eyes were full with the tears she had held back in Bec's presence. Clay pulled up a chair for her next to his. He wanted desperately to take her in his arms and comfort her, promise her anything to stop those tears. But he forced himself to sit back down in his chair and assume the only role that Sylvie wanted him to play, that of friend, confidant.

"I just don't understand," she moaned wiping her eyes.

"What don't you understand?" Clay asked patiently.

"Why can't he see that we were meant to be together?" she pleaded. "Always!" she added twisting the knife a little deeper into Clay's heart.

"Why don't you just start from the beginning," Clay tried to soothe her.

"Well, we were talking about relationships—just in general I mean—and somehow we started talking about marriage and I said I thought we'd make a good couple," she stopped here to wipe her eyes again. "Bec just laughed like he thought I was joking. When I told him I was serious he got upset and walked out. I just don't understand him. I know he loves me as much as I love him," she whimpered.

Clay tried to calm her offering the most reassuring cliches he could muster. Obviously her lover's image of Bec did not include that facet of his personality that balked at reins and fences. Clay wanted to tell Sylvie that he himself was capable of and longed for that commitment that Bec couldn't face. But as always he kept his feelings to himself. Sylvie seemed troubled enough. He didn't want to upset her further. After some time spent dabbing at her eyes and listening to Clay's platitudes about people and relationships Sylvie seemed calmer.

"Why don't we go out for an early dinner. Do you good to get out for a while," Clay suggested.

"Well, I don't know..." Sylvie looked doubtful.

"Bec probably won't be back for a while," he added guessing the reason for her indecision.

"Oh, I guess it would be all right then," she brightened.

Braeden's was almost empty at that hour. In fact they had only just opened for dinner and Clay and Sylvie were the first ones in the door. They chose a comfortable booth at the rear of the restaurant.

"This reminds me of our lunch meetings," Sylvie smiled.

"Yes, except it's not Wednesday," Clay returned her smile. Sylvie laughed softly remembering.

"You've always been able to help me, to make me feel better. It seems like I've known you for so much longer than it's actually been. You know I really missed you when I was in Seattle," the mention of the city sent a slight cloud over the pale face. 'She missed me,' Clay thought. Why couldn't it have been as one misses a lover not a sorority sister one confides in. Well, no matter, at least for the present precious hour Sylvie was with him not with Bec. Clay had her physical presence across the table from him even if her thoughts were elsewhere. For the moment that would have to do. Sylvie prattled on throughout the meal mostly about Bec naturally. By the time dessert came she had cheered herself up considerably.

"Well, I'll just go back to the house tonight and talk to him. No, maybe I won't say anything tonight—maybe tomorrow," Sylvie plotted her strategy. "I know eventually he'll see things the same way I do. He just has to!" she added confidently.

Clay nodded noncommittally. Perhaps it was just his memory playing tricks on him, Clay thought, but the suspicion surfaced again that there was an ineffable difference between the Sylvie sitting across from him now and the Sylvie of the Wednesday meetings. A certain subtlety of feeling seemed to be missing. Her emotions now appeared more basic—the tears, the laughter, the optimism of the child. Sitting in that booth staring across at the features that had etched themselves into his brain Clay was struck by a new possibility. This obsession with Bec—could Sylvie be crazy? And if so, where did that leave Clay with his obsessive longing for her. 'Perhaps we can share a padded cell somewhere,' Clay laughed inwardly, gloomily. He rose to help her on with her jacket. A cloud of hyacinths threatened to buckle his knees but he managed to recover and pay the check.

Presumably Sylvie decided to delay having another serious talk with Bec as the rest of the week passed serenely. The two were back on lovey-dovey status and Clay was trying hard not to listen through the wall.

On Saturday evening Michael stopped by the house. He had gone out of town soon after his birthday party. This was the first time he had seen Sylvie. He congratulated her on her apparent effect on Bec. In truth, Bec did now seem very close to the convivial, easy-going man he had been a few months before. Clay wondered how happy Michael would be if he knew what Sylvie had planned for Bec's future.

Pete stopped by, too, for a short visit on his way home to Polly. He had talked to Sylvie several times since her appearance in Trident Beach. Although polite, it was clear he did not share Michael's enthusiasm for the influence she was having on Bec. Pete had whispered at one point to Clay that he thought there was something strange about Sylvie though he couldn't say just exactly what. Perhaps Pete's instincts were right, Clay thought. When Bec and Michael left for the Westside alone Clay knew that Sylvie was disappointed not to have been included. She managed to cover it well until everyone left. Then as usual she turned to Clay for comfort.

"Well, you know—boys' night out," Clay offered.

"Yes, I suppose so," Sylvie sulked. "I was hoping that Bec and I could have a quiet evening, just the two of us, and maybe talk about our plans. But I guess it will just have to wait," she said glumly. And as usual Clay did his best to cheer her up.

Clay and Sylvie sat up reading and watching television until past midnight. Sylvie finally gave up and went to bed convinced by Clay that Bec was probably at Michael's, had lost track of the time, etc... Clay heard Bec come home around three in the morning. He wondered sleepily just how far Bec had returned to his old self.

Sunday was a cloudy, windswept day. The intermittent drizzle and breeze coming off the rough sea made the air feel much cooler than the thermometer reading. The weather seemed to mirror Clay's mood. He felt he had to spend the day with Janny. He had broken a date with her the night before in order to console Sylvie. It occurred to Clay that he had been using Janny in much the same way that Sylvie used him, for comfort and consolation. However, his growing sense of guilt made it increasingly difficult to spend time with Janny. And Janny was beginning to sense that there was something wrong, that something had come between them. In her usual candid fashion she came right out and asked Clay what it was. But he was unwilling—unable to tell her and so it was left hanging there unspoken between them.

When Clay arrived back at Bec's house Sunday evening it appeared that Sylvie had not had a much better day than he. She met him at the front door where she had obviously been awaiting his return. She seemed agitated though trying hard to control it.

"Where's Bec?" Clay asked.

"He left," she said firmly as if that explained everything.

"Did you two have another talk?" Clay guessed at the reason for Bec's departure.

"Yes, he just won't listen. I know if he would just listen I could make him understand," she sputtered letting off steam now that Clay was there. As before Clay comforted her, calmed her down although it took more doing this time than it had in the past. Sylvie had worked herself almost into hysterics waiting in the house alone. Clay couldn't help wondering what might have happened if Bec had been the first one to return rather than Clay. What would Bec have thought of this Sylvie, teary-eyed and whining?

Finally, cried-out, Sylvie went to bed early leaving Clay alone in the living room of the old house. Having used so much of his own energy to calm Sylvie and restore her equilibrium he felt drained, bled. He needed some fresh air and he also didn't want to hear whatever might pass between Sylvie and Bec when Bec returned home. The beach seemed the answer.

Memorial Day was still a week away but the town was filling up quickly. Each weekend in April and May brought more people, more traffic, more noise. On Saturdays and Sundays now the center of town was actually crowded. 'A taste of things to come,' Bec had told Clay talking about summer in full swing. And now in the evenings Clay noticed the few lighted outposts of winter residences between Bec's and the outer fringes of the town's center had turned into an almost unbroken string of porch lights and glowing front windows. Striding toward the beach Clay had to wait for several cars to pass—unheard of a few months before. Through the dark, misty air Clay felt he could actually sense the level of human activity rising in the small town. In the past he had shied away from densely populated areas. But somehow the idea of the hoards preparing to descend on the summer shore didn't upset him. They seemed to go along with the warming weather, a natural part of the changing seasons. He might have to wait a little longer for a table at Braeden's and his walks along the beach might not be quite so solitary but soon the air and the water would be warm enough to truly welcome him.

These thoughts occurred to Clay as he stood at the ocean's edge trying to find the horizon's break between black water and black sky. He made himself think about how nice it would be to walk to the beach early each morning and take a swim before starting in on the day's writing and typing. The possibility of really getting to know the sea firsthand. He made himself think about the boardwalk at the town's center. How warm and crowded and perhaps festive it would seem in high summer. Anything to keep from thinking about Sylvie. Her demands on him as confidant and consoler were taking their toll. Clay wasn't sure how much longer he could keep up the charade. As he walked back toward Bec's house he wondered who might break first, Sylvie or himself.

Clay had intended to stay away longer but the mist had turned into an honest-to-goodness rain. His thin jacket was soon soaked through and the biting edge of unseasonably cold air off the water added briskness to his steps as he turned from the ocean. As he approached the house Clay thought about getting in his car and going somewhere, anywhere to avoid Sylvie or worse Sylvie and Bec. But he was wet to the skin by now and shivering despite his pace.

Half a block away Clay spotted an unfamiliar car pulling up at the curb in front of Bec's house. Despite his discomfort Clay slowed his step a bit to see what was happening. In the streetlight's dim glow he saw Bec emerge from the passenger side and walk around to talk to the driver. He leaned in through the driver's window for what Clay determined was more than just a friendly good night. As the car passed him Clay could see the driver was a pretty, blond girl but no one he recognized. Bec starting up the walk saw Clay on his way toward the house.

"What are you doing out in this rain?" Bec laughed. "You look like a drowned rat," he added as Clay got closer.

"Well, you know what they say about someone who won't come in out of the weather. New friend?" Clay asked in spite of himself motioning with his soggy head toward the departing car.

"Just someone I met up on the boardwalk the other day. Nice girl," Bec answered casually. As the two walked up the front steps together Clay wondered what time it was and if Sylvie had witnessed the scene at the curb. Luckily the house was quiet as they entered.

"I'm going up and get out of these wet clothes," Clay checked the hall clock. "After eleven—guess I'll hit the sack. Oh, Sylvie said she was going to bed early."

"Ah..." Bec mumbled thoughtfully.

"See you in the morning," Clay started up the stairs.

"Yeah, right—morning..." Bec seemed preoccupied as he wandered off into the living room not the bedroom Clay noted with a sigh of relief.

Bec seemed to be returning to his old self. Clay wondered what this would mean for Sylvie. Bec had been willing to lean on her at a low point in his life but now that he was better? Of course Clay would secretly applaud a break between Sylvie and Bec but he hated the thought of her being hurt as he knew she would be. 'Perhaps,' Clay thought on the edge of sleep, 'perhaps I can find that small space between Bec and Sylvie and insinuate myself there like a wedge. To be there when she needs me, to lessen the hurt. A wedge, yes, start trying to be a wedge...tomorrow...' he thought drowsily.

CHAPTER XXIX

The rain continued off and on during the night. Clay could hear it beating at the large, round windows of his room as he turned over in his sleep. It continued while he spent the morning busy in Bec's writing room. Finally at lunchtime he could stand it no longer. Shedding shoes and socks and rolling up his pant legs Clay took an old umbrella from the hall closet and set off into the deluge. The wind had died during the night and now the rain came down straight and steady. Clay found it easy walking, the umbrella protecting the upper half of his body only his legs and feet getting soaked. He discovered the dichotomy to be physically pleasing—dry on top, wet on the bottom. The air had warmed and even the water falling about him was not as cold as he had expected. Mesmerized by the beat of the droplets Clay walked on. It was good to be out of the house. Sylvie had spent the morning sulking in the living room because Bec went off somewhere with Michael. Clay had retreated to the writing room. Although Bec seemed to be returning to his old self in every other way his interest in writing had not resurfaced since Arnie's death. Clay was secretly, selfishly relieved. He did not relish the idea of having to give up this new-found role.

Without realizing it Clay found he had walked almost to the center of town. Here the heavy rain and the naturally high water table were waging war against the storm drains. As he crossed the street Clay waded through the backup washing over the rounded, low curbs at the intersection. He stopped at the corner of James and Fourth Streets for a moment to peek out from underneath the large umbrella. The streets were nearly deserted owing to the weather. Nevertheless, Clay could feel the town steadily swelling and building toward summer. He knew there was something inside him building just as surely. He still loved Sylvie, was still obsessed with her but he was finding it increasingly difficult to spend time with her. Clay hated the crying and carrying on about Bec and still her refusal to speak of the husband and child she had left in Seattle as if they existed no more for her. How much longer could any of them go on like this—Sylvie, Bec or Clay? Reluctantly Clay turned back toward the house and the afternoon. Perhaps he could keep Sylvie at arm's length by holing up in the writing room again pleading a deadline. 'At arm's length,' Clay laughed ironically to himself, when all he had wanted was to take her in his arms.

Entering the house Clay sensed something was different. The music. Sylvie, rummaging through Bec's old albums had come up with the Doors' premiere. In Clay's absence she had somehow convinced herself that Bec would be home soon and everything would be all right. Clay subdued an urge to take her firmly by the shoulders and shake her into reality. Instead he retreated again to the typewriter. At least she wasn't crying he thought dismally. In fact, Bec didn't return for many hours and when he did was more than a little tipsy. But he was in a good mood and Sylvie managed to jolly him along into the bedroom. Whether they would fight or love Clay didn't want to hear and escaped out the front door into the night.

The rain had lessened to a mist and then stopped altogether in late afternoon. The sidewalks still damp glistened in the glow of the streetlights. Rather than heading for the beach Clay turned as he had earlier in the day for the center of town with no particular destination in mind. After a few blocks Clay turned west for a block on Twenty-first Street then back toward town on Astor Avenue. He had found this a pleasant walk on many occasions. It was the only truly tree-lined street in town with its slightly stunted but stately sycamores on both sides for most of its length. These and the close proximity of the houses to each other and to the sidewalk gave the street a closed-in, homey feel. This was the first time Clay had walked down it at night since spring had returned leaves to the old trees. A healthy breeze rustled the foliage beneath the streetlights' glow casting dancing shapes of pale yellow and black on the sidewalks below. The shadows of the leaves and tree trunks lengthened into narrow black corridors between the houses. The only sound as Clay passed was the chatter of the wind through the leaves. Only that sound and the darkness. No people, no cars. In other circumstances they might have seemed sinister, the shifting shadows. But to Clay tonight there was a magical quality to it all. He listened and watched as he walked as if the play of light and shadow and rustling leaves were a show put on just for his benefit. He let his mind free to wander. Inevitably it returned like a homing pigeon to Sylvie. Perhaps if he told her how he felt. She seemed to be changing or maybe he was just seeing her differently or getting to know her better. Not everything he learned pleased him but still he wanted her. But what did he really want of her? Certainly not the comfortable caring of Janny. No, it was something beyond that, even perhaps beyond sex, beyond love. Some deeper, darker need that he couldn't put a name to. And what about Sylvie? Did she never think of her abandoned husband and child? Did she ever think of anyone but Bec? Or did Bec dominate Sylvie's thoughts as she dominated Clay's own? Perhaps he would find a way to tell her tomorrow. By the time he returned to the house Clay had convinced himself that he had no choice but to confront Sylvie the next day and tell her how he really felt. The house lay mercifully quiet as he climbed the stairs to his room. He went to bed full of resolve for what he had decided must take place tomorrow.

The next morning Clay awoke to bright sunshine and a very stiff breeze rattling the windows of his room. Dressing with more care than usual he planned what he would say to Sylvie, how he might begin. The house was quiet. No one in the living room nor kitchen. Maybe they were sleeping late Clay thought. Then he found the reason in a note attached to the coffee pot. It said that Bec and Sylvie had gone to Atlantic City for the day and would probably not be back until late. Clay read the note over twice. He couldn't believe it. Now, when he had made the decision, had built himself up to the point of being able to confront Sylvie. 'Is somebody trying to tell me something?' he wondered.

Clay's initial feelings of anger and frustration quickly gave way to total deflation as he shuffled about the kitchen dazed, instinctively filling the coffee pot. What the hell was he supposed to do now? Since no other answer presented itself Clay wandered into the writing room but he found he couldn't concentrate. The wind was coming in steady gusts against the front of the house. He resisted the idea of escaping to the beach knowing he really should work. Then he came up with a compromise. Grabbing the typewriter he wrestled it up the stairs to his room. Clay opened each of the large, round windows as well as the long windows at the end of the hallway. Propping the door to his room open, the effect was complete—a wind that literally whistled through the house. After anchoring loose papers and clothing Clay sat down to the typewriter. The breeze was cool but not cold and Clay found it invigorating. He set to work. At least as long as he was writing he wouldn't have to think about anything else. Besides, it was simple—excepting the ability to write, Bec was recovering while Clay sank deeper. Bec was getting better and he had Sylvie's full attention.

Clay worked on in his room throughout the day until the breeze died at sunset. From the front porch he watched the clouds float like giant wisps of pink cotton candy, a luminescence moving with them as if somehow, impossibly they were lighted from within. As the last of the clouds disappeared from view Michael's silver Mercedes pulled up at the curb.

"So, where is everybody?" he asked coming up the walk his tone almost cheerful.

"Just me I'm afraid. Bec and Sylvie went to Atlantic City for the day. Won't be back 'til late."

"Jesus Christ!" The change in Michael's attitude was immediate. "What does he see in that girl? Can you tell me that? What does he see in her?"

Clay shrugged noncommittally. When Sylvie had first appeared in Trident Beach Michael was glad of her influence and help in bringing Bec out of his slump. Now, however, it was obvious his opinion of her was changing. He found her mood swings and her demands on Bec's time irritating and unnecessary and he said as much. She had served her purpose—now why didn't she just move along—or why didn't Bec tell her to go? Michael ranted on for a few moments, more to himself than to Clay. Finally, turning to go Michael asked Clay, "So, what do you think of her? You've spent more time with her. What's she really after?" Clay was tongue-tied. What could he say? He considered as Michael drove away. Was that what Sylvie intended, to separate Bec from his friends, to claim all his time and attention? Apparently Michael thought so. After all he hadn't been by to clean house in ages.

Bec and Sylvie returned after Clay had gone to bed. He could hear them moving around in the living room below, laughing and talking. It seemed they had had a good day. So where did that leave him? His determination to tell all to Sylvie had faded with the day.

Clay decided he would just have to wait and see what morning brought.

CHAPTER XXX

Morning brought a brilliant sunrise, a tantalizing part of which Clay could see from the front windows of his room. Impulsively he wanted a better look at it. Dressing quickly he crept down the stairs of the still quiet house and out the front door. When he reached the beach Clay found he was not alone. The spectacular sunrise had attracted several onlookers. Even a couple of joggers had stopped in mid-run to take it in. A gray-white cloud—long and narrow, knife-shape but dense cloaked the sun's passage from sea to sky. Like the curtains at the wings of a giant stage thought Clay. The sun quickly rose from the cloud, the major part of it gleaming free before being barred by a series of wisps which it turned to gold as it passed upward. Instinctively, Clay closed his eyes and breathed deeply as if to capture its essence. He had forgotten how fast the sun moves when so close to the horizon. Soon it was well on its way, the clouds and the onlookers dispersed. Clay found himself momentarily alone on the beach. What to do? Go back to the house and confront Sylvie as he had planned the day before? Go back and say nothing, just continue on in the same tortured way? No, Clay really didn't want to do either. He really didn't know what he wanted. Time perhaps? Yes, that might help. Time to take a step back and think. As he had accomplished more than usual at the typewriter the day before, Clay decided to take the day off to try to sort things out in his mind. Hell, he wouldn't even go back to the house and tell anyone. Let them wonder where he was. 'Right!' thought Clay bitterly, 'they probably won't even notice that I'm not there.' Shaking off this last thought he headed north up the beach a few blocks to where the long boardwalk started.

This part of the boardwalk was free, unencumbered on both sides. The beach and the ocean to his right as he walked toward the center of town, the houses on the left keeping their distance behind stubby bulkheads and pilings, the guardians of hurricane season. Clay found he'd picked a good day to play hooky. The sun climbing through a sky of deepening blue quickly warmed the air. Soon Clay had to shed the light jacket he had worn out at sunrise. How ironic thought Clay that he had chosen this day, a Wednesday, to put some distance between Sylvie and himself. He remembered how he had looked forward to Wednesdays as the only days when he could spend a little time with her. Continuing down the boardwalk Clay felt a pang of guilt as he passed Janny's place. He knew she would already have left for the day but he hurried by just the same. He had broken a date with her the night before for no good reason. Since Sylvie's reappearance he had seen less and less of Janny. Clay didn't know what to do about that any more than he knew what to do about Sylvie. Maybe if he could just set them both aside for the day and enjoy himself. Was that possible? He could try.

Clay paced along the narrow, weathered boards. He noticed the beach was dotted now with the tall, rickety-looking stands that would soon hold lifeguards on regular duty, who, he was given to understand by Bec, were a breed unto themselves. He walked on past block after block of the low-slung beachfront houses. With May came the expected students escaping after final exams but also families with small children and pets in tow and older couples as well. An established, moveable community that came and went with the seasons. Generation after generation following as a matter of course as if to spend the summer elsewhere would be literally unthinkable, as if the thought could never enter their minds. Unlike some summer towns which changed radically during 'the season' Trident Beach's true character seemed to take shape, to flesh out gradually with warm weather. This was not just a place for wild flings by vacationing students, it was basically a family town. While some seasonal towns seemed to become more unstable with the influx of visitors, Trident Beach appeared to grow more solid as they arrived.

Clay felt he had come to know the town, to witness its special secrets unfolding before him with the changing times of day and season. Occasionally he had considered going back to North Carolina or somewhere else to try to escape Sylvie's spell. But he knew he couldn't do that now. His center of gravity had shifted to become firmly anchored in the coarse, yellow sand of the South Jersey shore. Clay realized that this town had gained at least as powerful a hold over him as had Sylvie. Even with the turmoil in his mind over Sylvie and Janny he was comforted by a feeling of finally belonging somewhere, of being glad of where he was rather than longing to be somewhere else. And besides, how could he think about leaving when Mr. Suey was due back from Florida next week. Clay looked forward to seeing the old man again, to telling him he had been right about a life by the sea.

Finally Clay came to the point a few blocks south of the center of town where the boardwalk widened and rose higher above the sand. Houses gave way here to commercial enterprises. With each weekend during spring more and more shops and restaurants had opened, like flowers coming into bloom under the watchful gaze of the sun. Now with Memorial Day weekend only a couple days away they had burst into full blossom. There was a party atmosphere to this part of the boardwalk, an air of anticipation for the weekend that would 'officially' kick off the summer season. The places that sold fudge and salt water taffy and pizza by the slice were all gearing up for the onslaught. Some of these were housed in narrow buildings whose lower facades retracted like large garage doors to leave the whole front of the shop open to the boardwalk. Everywhere paint had been retouched and signs redone after the ravages of the winter winds. Clay noticed that the little shop that sold freshly baked coconut macaroons had opened. He skirted it remembering the story Pete had told him of becoming sick from eating too many of the cookies washed down with birch beer. He stopped instead at a place that made the best orange drink he'd ever had. He watched the operation behind the counter as he finished his drink. Bushels of fresh oranges awaited the squeezers and giant tubs where their juice would be mixed with just the right amounts of sugar and water and stirred by a burly, gray-haired man with a long, wooden paddle.

It was mid-morning when Clay reached the point where Fourth Street dead-ended at the boardwalk. Here the boards were quite high off the sand. Clay stopped for a while to lean against the railing and look out over the beach and the small waves breaking at the water's edge. It was a sight he knew he would never tire of. Turning back to continue his walk toward the north end of town Clay noticed a sign proclaiming the opening of the movie theater at the corner of Second Street and the boardwalk. He made a mental note. If nothing else he wanted to see the inside of the old theater. The idea of being able to walk straight from the boards into a movie theater somehow intrigued him.

A few blocks past the center of town the boardwalk veed to the west playing nip and tuck around a few small shops and an aging hotel before coming to an end in a long, sloping ramp. Clay decided to continue north following much the same path as when he first explored the town on Bec's old bicycle. The beaches grew narrower at this end of town—thin, yellow strips cut by an occasional rock jetty and banked by high, broad dunes. Tucked behind the dunes and just east of The Greens was another residential area where Michael's house was located. These were mostly the summer homes of the wealthy. This was unlike most of the carefully laid-out town. The streets here ran short and chock-a-block as if the whole neighborhood had been an afterthought.

The narrow streets were lined with parked cars now where a few months earlier there had been almost none. Clay appreciated Trident Beach's split personality. The well-ordered layout of the town's center and south end versus the hodgepodge array at the northern tip, the shift between summer and the off-season. They seemed to mirror the division in Clay's mind—Sylvie versus Janny.

Clay found an access to the beach, a well-worn slit cut between dunes. A light breeze feathered the sparse dune grass. Clay stood at the ocean's edge. Although the water was still quite cool there were a few brave souls bobbing up and down with the gentle swells. Clay had promised himself that next week, cold or not, he was going in the water. He had built this up in his mind almost to the point of some sort of mystical challenge. Gazing north to where the shoreline curved out in a slight bulge before dipping back in toward The Greens, Clay could just make out the ancient, narrow toll bridge spanning the tiny inlet between Trident Beach and the next small town up the coast. From there the shoreline curved away in a sharp crescent sliver capped by the water tower at Longport.

As he was becoming ravenously hungry, Clay decided to postpone his planned tour of The Greens. Besides, he told himself, in that predominantly year-round neighborhood probably little changed with the advent of summer. Heading back toward the center of town Clay turned away from the beach. Passing the library and surrounding older Victorian-style guest houses Clay picked up the alley way that ran directly behind Columbus Street. Here he found that spring had brought changes as well. More activity was evident though indicated mostly by the sound level rising behind the fences. A veritable battalion of garbage cans lined the narrow, concrete corridor now. There was a faint sweet-sour smell that Clay discovered was unique to warm weather and the few blocks of alley way behind several old restaurants in the middle of town.

Clay enjoyed a leisurely lunch at The Sandspur, a tiny place on Strayport Road between Second and Third Streets. There were only four small wooden booths and a dozen stools at a narrow counter in what had once been the living room of the old house. The place had been open during weekends for the past few weeks but now it was full-time. The couple who ran it were both teachers at a local community college Clay learned. They had spent the last several summers like this, doing something they found both profitable and enjoyable. Clay envied them their enthusiasm and sense of togetherness. As he finished his lunch Clay caught a glimpse of the reason the food tasted like it had just been cooked by someone's mother. In fact it had. In the tiny kitchen a wiry, gray-haired woman bustled about a stove not much bigger than the one at Bec's house. Her smile and energetic movements bespoke an attitude akin to the couple behind the counter. Leaving, Clay wondered if the happy, little family lived in the small bungalow in back of the diminutive restaurant and wondered who did the cooking when they were off duty. He knew he'd be back. The cooking and the cozy atmosphere would make the long walk from Bec's worthwhile.

After lunch Clay retraced his steps to the library where he spent the balance of the afternoon lolling about the magazine racks indulging himself in reading about whatever happened to catch his eye. Around five o'clock he decided it was time to turn back toward Bec's, but he was in no hurry. Stopping at the aging department store on Columbus Street in the middle of town Clay carefully selected a pair of swimming trunks for his coming adventure. After a couple slices of pizza at Mackie's on the boardwalk Clay headed west on Fourth Street, then south again. He noticed that most of the seafood places along Columbus Street had opened their doors now. He saw a couple college-age boys eating take-out food sitting on the sidewalk their backs propped against the brick facade of one of the older buildings. The hotels and rentals were all opening now from the high-dollar ones near the beach to the medium-range bungalows a couple blocks back to the Oceanic at Sixth Street and Brigantine Avenue. This last Clay had been given to understand was just a cut above a flophouse. He couldn't help but laugh to himself when he came upon a young man, probably a college student fresh from finals. The youth was leaning over the open trunk of his car busily rooting around in an untidy suitcase. Presently he found what he was after. It was a small can of spray deodorant which he proceeded to apply there on the spot to his underarms, reaching up under his shirt to accomplish this. Seeming well-pleased with himself, he slammed the trunk lid and took off down the sidewalk. Probably getting ready for a hot date Clay smiled to himself. Clay had to admit that the warm weather had brought with it an influx of pretty, young girls. They were everywhere in their white waitress uniforms, the color of their aprons indicating where they worked. And once in a while, the delicious black uniforms with lacy, white aprons of the chambermaids from The Sussex, the ritzy, old hotel on the boardwalk just off the center of town. He almost wished he were free to enjoy them. This thought made him sad and he turned unconsciously back toward the alley ways but he found no comfort there. From an open window at the back of a sagging three-story house Clay overheard the poignant anguish of a couple breaking up. He could just make out the man's muffled pleas but the woman's voice was clear though tremulous. "I just can't do it for you anymore!" she cried over and over. Clay scurried on his way, the pain in the woman's voice hitting too close to home.

Clay felt the day away had done him good. By the time he got back to Bec's house he was certain of two things. He wanted to continue this life he had built for himself in Trident Beach. He also wanted Sylvie. The only problem now was how to merge these two desires into one coherent possibility. All along Clay had imagined that if Sylvie knew how much he cared for her and how little she really meant to Bec she would of course turn to Clay. But what if this was not the case? What if instead she went running back to her husband? Either way, Clay had to find out. The first step must be a serious talk with Sylvie. Maybe he would even talk to her tonight. He decided to see what the atmosphere was like at Bec's.

CHAPTER XXXI

The atmosphere at Bec's was calm. Steely Dan poured fluidly from the stereo. Bec sat alone in the living room, Sylvie having gone to bed early. When he first entered the room, Clay thought Bec was asleep. He sat in one of the old armchairs, his head leaning back over the top of the chair as if he had dozed off. But as Clay approached he saw that Bec's eyes were open, fixed as if studying the ceiling.

"I've been waiting for you," Bec said almost in a whisper presumably not wanting to wake Sylvie.

"Yeah, sorry I kind of disappeared today—I just needed some time to myself," Clay responded in the same low tone. Bec shook his head as if to dismiss this.

"No problem. That's not what I want to talk to you about," his face had an uncharacteristic seriousness about it. "Come on, let's go for a walk on the beach. I don't want to take a chance on having Sylvie overhear us." Though his legs were tired from the day's walk, Clay followed silently out the front door. Whatever Bec had to say it seemed important.

A terrible thought hit Clay as they crossed Ocean Boulevard before reaching the beach. Had Bec learned of Clay's erstwhile work as a private investigator? Had

Sylvie told him? Halfway to the water's edge Bec stopped and turned to face Clay. Clay tried to prepare himself for whatever might follow.

"It's Sylvie," Bec began. "I just don't know what the hell to do about her." Clay held his breath and let Bec continue. "It's been nice having her around for a while. I mean I'm grateful to her for the time she spent with me after Arnie...you know. It's just that now," here Bec threw up his hands in a gesture of helplessness, "now it's time to move on but she doesn't get the message. With other women I've known they seem to be able to sense when a thing has leveled out and they back off, but not Sylvie." Shoving his hands deep in his pockets Bec turned and started walking slowly south down the beach. Following at his side Clay decided the best course for the moment was just to be an attentive listener.

"Sylvie just seems to want more and more," Bec continued. "Not things, I mean, or money—nothing like that. She wants more of me, more of my time. We spent that whole day together in Atlantic City, right? I figured maybe that'd keep her happy for a while, kind of appease this hunger to spend time with me. But did that work? Hell, no! It just whetted her appetite for more. Now she thinks we should spend every day and every night together. Christ!—she keeps talking about marriage. I don't want to hurt her feelings but I just have to get out of this some way."

"So you want me to talk to her?" Clay asked trying to guess why Bec was confiding all this to him.

"No, I'll do that myself. It's the least I can do. I do need a favor from you though," he stopped again looking out toward the black water.

"What is it?" Clay asked hesitantly.

"I'm going to talk to Sylvie but I'd like to put it off until this weekend is over."

"Why? What's happening this weekend?"

"Well, it's Memorial Day weekend—beginning of summer and everything. Anyway, Michael and I decided to organize a party. Actually it was Michael's idea. Haven't had a party at the house for a while. It'll be kind of nice to get a little life in the old place again."

"Does Sylvie know about the party?"

"Yeah, she thinks it's a great idea—celebrate the holiday and all."

"You said something about a favor?"

"Oh, yeah. Look, I know it's asking a lot. You seem to get along pretty well with Sylvie. Do you think you could spend some time with her, kind of keep an eye on her between now and Saturday night when we have the party?"

"I—ah," Clay stammered, astonished.

"I know it's a lot to ask, but if you could just help keep things on an even keel 'til after the party?" Bec asked hopefully.

"Ah—yeah, sure I'll do what I can," Clay answered recovering as best he could, grateful the darkness hid the surprise on his face.

"Great—that's great. I really appreciate it Clay. Look, I've been meaning to thank you for something else, too."

"What's that?"

"The way you've taken over the writing for me—it's really kept me out of a bind."

"I don't mind. Actually, I'm enjoying it," Clay admitted sheepishly.

"That's good because it looks like the muse has decided to take an extended vacation. I really don't know when I'll feel like writing again."

"Don't worry about it. I've got it covered," Clay reassured him.

"You've really been a help, Clay. I guess it's a good thing you came along when you did." 'Yeah, a lucky coincidence,' thought Clay as they turned back the way they had come.

Alone in his room Clay thought about what Bec had said. Clay was not surprised that the party was Michael's idea. No doubt his way of coming between Bec and Sylvie. There hadn't been a party in the house since Arnie's death, not since Sylvie's arrival. Clay guessed that Michael was hoping the rowdy gathering would be too much for her. Clay could scarcely believe what he had heard. Bec wanted him to spend time with Sylvie until he had a chance to let her down easily? What more could Clay ask? This was the opportunity he needed. If he could just keep quiet for a few more days. But still, he was here in his room alone while downstairs Bec lay beside Sylvie. Just a few more days.

Bec was up and out early the next morning leaving Clay to his task of coping with Sylvie. This proved both easier and more difficult than Clay had imagined. He had been afraid that she would be at loose ends, need shepherding through the day. Quite the contrary, she proved very self-sufficient. Excited about the party, she had taken it upon herself to give the house a good spring cleaning. What Clay found challenging was being in such close proximity to her without being able to tell all. After a few moments alone with her he found himself biting his tongue, having to swallow the words he wanted so desperately to say. He managed to handle the situation by spending most of the day in the writing room, appearing every hour or so to move a heavy piece of furniture or render an opinion on the placement of a chair.

Clay had never seen Sylvie so animated, so lively. She had swept her dark hair back from her face into a small ponytail. She seemed paler than usual despite the physical effort she was making. Her eyes gleamed with the excitement of anticipation. Clay watched as she scurried about the house to the beat of The Doors album which she insisted on playing over and over. It was almost frightening in a way. She seemed so different from the timid, soft-spoken woman Clay had met in his Uncle Bert's office. He feared that Sylvie envisioned a different sort of party than the one that would in all likelihood take place. He gathered she thought it would be a chance for her to get to know a few of Bec's friends. Clay wondered if she realized just how many friends Bec had.

The next day, Friday, was much the same. Bec was up and out early, again, making himself as scarce as possible for the rest of the day. Clay guessed he was probably at the Westside with Michael, or curled up somewhere with a new blonde. Sylvie set to work on the kitchen, the music of The Doors debut album echoing throughout the house, again. Clay found himself missing the music Bec had played for his other women—Marianne's favorite Eric Carmen album, Van Morrison for the mystery ladies. By the end of the day, Clay seriously considered either hiding or breaking the album Sylvie had fixated on. Its dark rhythms seemed to reflect his growing torment at having to be so close to her and yet remain silent. The only bright spot came when Clay discovered that Janny had to work Saturday and so would not be able to attend the party. He had been putting her off for several days and had out of guilt reluctantly invited her. He was much relieved when he learned she would not be able to come. Finally late that evening Bec returned home and the restorative strains of Steely Dan flowed through the house. 'Just another day or two,' thought Clay.

Clay was relieved Saturday morning when Bec took Sylvie in hand himself. The two of them went off to buy beer and nibbles for the party leaving Clay to blissful silence in the empty house. Around two o'clock Bec dropped off Sylvie and the refreshments and went out again pleading some personal errand. Clay could guess what. Sylvie's nervousness was getting the better of her. She was desperate that Bec's friends should approve of her, unaware that she had already alienated two of Bec's closest friends, Michael and Pete. Finally Clay insisted that she accompany him for a walk on the beach hoping it might relax her a bit.

It was without a doubt the warmest day so far, just a shade away from downright hot. The flat, yellowed, concrete sidewalks on the way to the beach radiated heat. The warmth rose up and closed around them as they walked toward the ocean. Hot, freshly-baked bread—that was what it reminded Clay of. They walked along the water's edge for perhaps an hour. Several times Clay almost opened up to Sylvie. But each time he thought to tell her, she began babbling again about some detail of preparation for the party.

The final straw came in late afternoon when Sylvie insisted Clay help her decide what to wear that evening. Protesting, Clay was dragged into the bedroom she and Bec shared and made to sit on the edge of the bed while she pulled several dresses from the closet. Clay tried not to let himself think that this was the bed which she shared with Bec. Whirling about, she held each dress up to herself in turn, waiting for Clay's assessment. He hadn't the heart to tell her that a pair of jeans and an old sweater would probably be more suitable. He didn't know how much of this he could stand. Beginning to feel like a harem eunuch, he fully expected her to start trying the dresses on in front of him at any moment. How could she be so unaware of his feelings as she paraded back and forth before the mirror, before him? He wanted desperately to make her feel what he was feeling. He wanted to reach out and pull her down, to make love to her in the middle of the pile of discarded dresses on Bec's bed. He was just about at the point of doing so when Bec appeared.

"Well, what's this? Has the party started early?" he laughed. "I didn't know it was going to be a costume ball," he joked pointing to Clay on the bed surrounded by a sea of women's clothing. "Oh, you mustn't look!"

Sylvie exclaimed trying to hide the scarlet dress she had a moment earlier held up for Clay's inspection.

"Why not?" Bec asked.

"Oh, I think it's bad luck or something," Sylvie sputtered.

"Don't be silly—that's just for weddings," Bec responded, a trace of irritation in his voice.

"Well, I think I'll go take a shower," Clay leapt to his feet seizing the opportunity to extricate himself from this scene.

"But you didn't tell me which one you liked best," Sylvie moaned.

"Oh, that last one—definitely," Clay called over his shoulder, nearly running from the room. Racing up the stairs as fast as he could, he almost felt he was going to be sick by the time he reached his room. He thought about skipping the party altogether but Bec had again specifically asked that he be there to keep an eye on Sylvie. If only Bec knew the emotional turmoil this was costing him. But in a very real way Clay felt he owed it to Bec. To somehow rectify, if only in his own mind, the deception that had first brought him into Bec's house. Clay took several deep breaths. At least there would be lots of other people around tonight. Perhaps that would make things easier.

CHAPTER XXXII

There were indeed lots of people. They started drifting in around seven-thirty. By eight o'clock a thick fog bank of cigarette smoke hung over the downstairs. Clay lost count of the faces coming and going but they all seemed to know Bec and he greeted each one in turn. At seven Sylvie had appeared in the living room to begin her anxious vigil until the arrival of the first guest. Clay noticed she was wearing the scarlet dress, the last one she had shown him—the one he had off-handedly told her he liked best. Actually he had to admit it suited her perfectly. The knit fabric hugged her slender body following every curve that Clay had dreamed of knowing. The color accentuated her pale skin and her dark, shining hair.

Clay tried to get Sylvie to sit down and relax but she was beside herself with nervousness. She paced restlessly back and forth across the worn living room carpet peering out the front windows. Bec was still in the shower and she was terrified that someone she didn't know might arrive before he was ready. When Bec finally appeared dressed in old jeans and an open-necked shirt, Sylvie fairly pounced on him, gripping his arm for reassurance. Bec cast a furtive glance at Clay that seemed to say, 'Oh, God!'.

When people started arriving Bec drifted off. Clay stuck close to Sylvie trying to soothe her by explaining that Bec had to play host so of course he couldn't spend all his time with her. As the evening progressed Bec managed to be in the kitchen when Sylvie was in the living room, in the hallway when she was in the kitchen. Clay led her around introducing her to people, those that he knew at any rate, trying to make her feel more comfortable. But her nervousness eventually gave way to irritated frustration as Bec kept eluding her.

Desperate to calm Sylvie, Clay offered her a can of beer. He knew it was probably a mistake, she wasn't much of a drinker. He just didn't know what else to do. He was running out of excuses for Bec. Sylvie downed two cans of beer in rapid succession and started in on a third. Whether out of nervousness or a desire to fit in Clay couldn't guess. He thought about stopping her but decided—what was the use? By the time the noise level reached a point that made conversation close to impossible Sylvie was beyond talking to anyway. Finally Clay sat her down in an armchair, trying to make himself comfortable perched on its arm. She sat dazed as the voices, music and smoked swirled about her. Occasionally she glanced up at Clay wonderingly and he gave her a reassuring smile. He thought this had to be the longest evening of his life.

At one point, Pete wandered over and tried to talk to Clay. It was difficult over the din but Clay gathered that Pete had not been around lately because he and his father had been especially busy with their exterminating business, obliging people wanting to have their houses sprayed before opening them for the summer. Clay guessed that Pete's disaffection for Sylvie was equally responsible for his absence from Bec's house. It was good to see Pete again. Clay hadn't realized how much he missed their talks.

As Clay turned back from Pete he saw someone handing Sylvie another beer. Before he could intervene she was swallowing in large gulps from the can, her eyes fixed straight ahead. 'Oh, God!' thought Clay, 'what if she gets sick?' When her head started to loll down toward her chest, Clay seized the opportunity. Propping her up, Clay walked her as nonchalantly as possible out of the living room. Sylvie offered no resistance. Supported by Clay she moved like a sleepwalker through the sea of strange faces. By the time Clay got her to the hallway her legs were beginning to give out. When they reached Bec's bedroom at the back of the house he was all but dragging her. As she fell from Clay's arms onto the bed he realized she was totally unconscious. He thought about undressing her but decided against it. Carefully placing a pillow beneath her head, he covered her with an old quilt. He turned back to look at her as he left the room. She looked like a child sleeping peacefully, her dark hair curling against the white pillowcase. She probably wouldn't remember much about the evening. Perhaps tomorrow he could even convince her that she had had a good time. At least she hadn't gotten sick Clay thought thankfully.

CHAPTER XXXIII

Clay sat alone in the living room amidst a host of empty beer cans and overflowing ashtrays. He welcomed the silence after the noise of the night before. Lazily leafing through the Sunday newspaper he watched the mid-morning sun trace patterns on the carpet. He guessed Sylvie and Bec must still be sleeping it off as he had not heard them go out. Perhaps this would be the day he could tell Sylvie. After the way Bec avoided her last night she had to see the futility of that relationship. That was, provided she remembered anything at all about last night. He would just have to wait and see what sort of shape she was in today.

Turning a page, Clay caught a glimpse of red out of the corner of his eye. Startled, he dropped the newspaper to the floor. Sylvie stood in the doorway from the kitchen. She was still wearing the scarlet dress from the night before though it was badly rumpled now. Her hair bespoke a night of heavy slumber. She took a few steps toward Clay and he jumped to his feet instinctively—something about her appearance very disturbing. He thought if her skin looked any more translucent he might be able to see right through it.

"Well, where is he?" she almost shouted, a bitter edge to her voice. Taken off-guard by this unexpected outburst Clay stood silent, dumbfounded before her.

"Well?" she asked impatiently.

"Who?" Clay finally managed.

"Who? Bec! Who do you think? Where is he?" she demanded, her eyes lighted by a ferocity that Clay found positively frightening.

"I don't know. I thought he was with you. I guess he must have gone out. I'm sure he'll be back soon. Do you want some coffee?" he asked trying to soothe her.

"No. Where is he?" she demanded again unreasonably.

"I told you I don't know, Sylvie," Clay answered trying to remain calm.

"I have to talk to him. I have to make him understand. He just doesn't understand," she seemed to be working herself up into some sort of frenzy.

"Understand what?" Clay asked patiently, striving to understand himself. Sylvie regarded him as one might a difficult child.

"That he has to spend more time with me, of course." Contrary to Clay's hopes, Bec's inattentiveness during the party had not dissuaded her but rather galvanized her in the opposite direction.

"He has to see that I'm the only one. The right one for him!" She was gesticulating wildly by now, and with her matted hair and flaming eyes seemed the archetypal madwoman. She was hardened, driven solely by her relentless need for Bec. Gone was the last vestige of the vulnerability which Clay had found so appealing. The scent of hyacinths that had fueled Clay's fantasies now seemed overpowering, cloying.

"As soon as he gets back we'll set a date for the wedding, then everything will be all right," she ranted on. Clay felt as if he had been swept into a vortex. He half-expected to hear the squeal of grinding metal at the collision of the image of Sylvie he had created for himself and the raving reality before him.

"Wedding date? Are you crazy?" Clay blurted out.

Sylvie gaped at him, unsure whether to be hurt or angry. But it was too late for smoothing over, for reassurances. Clay could feel the pressure of the months of hope and frustration pushing words to the front of his mind and out of his mouth. It was too late now. The sluice gate had been opened and the captive emotions tumbled forth carried on the flood current.

"Are you so completely blind that you can't see what's going on around here?" he shouted at her. Dumbstruck, Sylvie moved her mouth as if to speak but Clay continued before she had the chance.

"Bec doesn't care anything about you. You were just a diversion at a low point in his life—a passing pleasure who's outstayed her welcome. I can't believe you don't see that." Incomprehension and hurt were crowding out the anger in Sylvie's eyes but still Clay kept on. He knew he was wounding her but he couldn't stop. Perhaps it was the only way he could make her feel anything at all for him, make her see the truth.

"No!" she finally burst in on him. "Why are you saying these things? I don't believe you!" she cried starting to turn toward the hallway. But Clay wasn't finished. Grabbing her by the wrist he whirled her around to face him.

"Believe it!" he said forcefully. Her anger returning, she tried to wriggle from his grasp but he held her fast as the words continued to pour from him. "It's the truth, Sylvie. He doesn't care about you, but I did. I had since the first day I met you." Clay felt his chest swell. His temples pounded with the rush of freedom—the words that were setting him free.

"I needed you, Sylvie. I loved you more than Bec ever could even if he wanted to. I wanted you, Sylvie. I dreamed of making love to you for months but all you could see was Bec." Sylvie put her free hand to her head as if unable to take all this in.

"Why are you saying all these things? I thought you were my friend, Clay. It can't be the truth."

"Truth?" Clay shouted bitterly. "Truth? I'll give you truth! You know why you're still wearing that goddamn red dress? Because I didn't trust myself to take it off you when I put you to bed last night. That's how much I wanted you!"

Her eyes wide with amazement, Sylvie seemed on the point of speaking when a loud giggle drew her attention. She paused, listening and the laughter came again from somewhere on the second floor. Sylvie wrenched free from Clay's grasp and made for the stairs. Clay started after her but was brought up short when he reached the hallway. Just outside the living room door he came face to face with Janny.

"How long have you been here?" he asked automatically but he needn't have. The look of hurt and betrayal in her eyes was answer enough. She moved to go.

"Janny, let me explain." At that moment, the front door opened and Pete appeared.

"Janny, wait!" Clay cried after her but it was too late. She had escaped through the open door.

"Trouble in paradise?" Pete ventured.

"Jeez, what a morning!" Clay threw up his hands in desperation. Before he could enlarge upon this, they heard the crash of shattering glass upstairs.

"Good God—now what?" Clay muttered angrily.

The breaking glass was followed by screams and another crash, much louder this time. Clay and Pete rushed to the second floor, taking the steps two at a time. Reaching the top of the stairs they saw that most of the glass and a good part of the wooden frame were missing from the window at the far end of the hall. Rushing to the window Clay and Pete were relieved to see that the only casualty on the patio outside below was an old chair that had stood in the hallway. A shrill voice drew their attention toward the bedroom to the left of the broken window. The shades were pulled down making it hard to see at first. As their eyes adjusted to the dim light Clay and Pete could see Sylvie standing over the bed screaming at Bec. Bec lay on the bed half-covered by a sheet. In a dark corner, a young, blonde girl clutched her clothes fearfully in front of her. Cringing, she looked as if she were hoping to disappear into the shadows.

"What the hell is going on?" Bec asked when he saw Clay and Pete. Before either could say a word, Sylvie began screaming louder and set upon Bec, pounding at him with her tiny fists.

"Jeez, what do we do now?" Pete asked. But they didn't have to worry about the answer to that question. Behind them, they could hear several sets of feet pounding on the stairs. Apparently the crashing glass and Sylvie's screams had caused a neighbor to call the police. Two uniformed officers pushed past Clay and Pete and quickly assessing the situation grabbed hold of Sylvie. By this time she was totally out of control screaming, crying, ranting incoherently. She tried to bite, scratch and kick the officers—anything to get free. They managed to wrestle her out of the room and down to a waiting squad car. A third policeman strongly suggested that Bec and his lady friend get dressed as quickly as possible and with Clay and Pete accompany them to the police station.

After much explaining and several comments by one of the officers that this was a hell of a way to start off the summer season, Clay, Pete, Bec and the blonde were released. Sylvie was to be transferred to a nearby hospital for evaluation. At Clay's suggestion, a call was put through to her husband in Seattle.

CHAPTER XXXIV

It was the first Sunday of June. It was exactly a week ago that the police had dragged Sylvie screaming from Bec's house. A week. It seemed more like a year, Clay thought, as he turned from the breakfast crowd at Braeden's toward the boardwalk. The air was warm although the sky was mostly overcast. Looking overhead Clay was startled to see a large rent in the clouds revealing a hollow of pure, deep blue. It seemed somehow unnatural—that blue without the sun. Walking the few blocks to the boardwalk Clay thought back over the past week. He heard Janny's voice. 'I don't really know what I expected of you—it just wasn't this,' she had said at their parting. There really was no way he could explain, so he let it go. She decided to go to New Hampshire where her brother lived, borrow some money from him and go to school full-time. It was probably for the best, Clay decided. Perhaps he could have been happy with Janny but it wouldn't have been fair only giving her a fraction of his mind, his love.

And he thought about Sylvie. Sylvie. It was hard now to believe she had had such a hold over him. After his blowup at Sylvie it was as if a giant carbuncle had been lanced, the vile fluid draining away as the long held-back words flowed from him. Now there was only a bitter emptiness when he thought of her. He remembered how she looked when the police dragged her from Bec's house. He wondered if she had changed or if he had finally seen her as she really was. Clay had been much relieved to learn that her husband had agreed to take her back and would see that she got the help she needed. Ironically he turned out to be a psychiatrist. 'Perfect,' thought Clay.

As for his short career as a private investigator, Sylvie was the only one who knew why and how Clay had first come to be in Trident Beach. She was safely back in Seattle and besides, who would believe anything she said now? It was hardly likely that Janny, even if she did return from New England, would ever reveal to Bec or any of his friends the scene she had witnessed between Clay and Sylvie. His new life might just be secure after all. It was not perfect, not seamless, this web of deception, but it just might hold together. At any rate it was a risk Clay was willing to take. In time he might even forget himself what had first brought him to Trident Beach. Besides, with his dream of Sylvie shattered what did he have to lose? And to gain? The continuance of his new identity and a life near the ocean which was exerting an ever-increasing influence over him. It was easy—'just keep on going and don't look back', he told himself.

Clay approached the boardwalk. It was still early enough that the walk was dominated by the traditional Sunday morning bicycle traffic. The tires thumped the boards lightly as they sped by. He dodged the spinning, silver wheels, southbound then northbound, to get to the railing overlooking the beach. Clay had come to the boardwalk to say goodbye. Bec, Michael and Pete were waiting for him at the railing. Pete was to drive Bec and Michael to the airport. The two were going to spend an indeterminate amount of time with Michael's mother in Paris. Bec's interest in writing had still not returned. He decided some time away was perhaps what he needed. In the interim, he had arranged for Clay to continue writing though now under his own pen name. Bec had also spoken to his mother. Clay was to look after the house and Mr. Suey and the other summer tenants who were now filling the second floor rooms.

"Just wanted to take a last look," Bec smiled gazing out over the sand to the water. Michael seemed happier, more congenial than Clay could remember. But perhaps that wasn't so strange, thought Clay. Michael had nothing to lose now, his influence over Bec would be complete.

Marianne had come, too, to say goodbye. Clay realized how much he had missed her presence around the house. Her smile seemed sweeter than ever. Pete, practical as always, reminded them it was time to go if they wanted to catch their flight. Turning from the railing Bec shook hands with Clay.

"Thanks for taking care of things for me, I appreciate it," he said seriously. Then a smile lighted his face and he was again the happy-go-lucky Bec whom Clay had met when he first came to Trident Beach. "Hey, just be happy, man! That's what it's all about, right?" Bec laughed clapping a hand on Clay's shoulder and then he and Michael and Pete were gone.

Clay turned back to Marianne. They strolled slowly arm-in-arm down the boardwalk toward Bec's house. 'Perhaps,' thought Clay, 'I might even play the Eric Carmen album for her.'

The End

www.ingramcontent.com/pod-product-compliance
Lightning Source LLC
Chambersburg PA
CBHW061119100726
47911CB00013B/600